"Darling, don't look so suspicious."

Claire's voice turned low and sultry. She reminded Tony of a cat closing in on its prey. "It'll be a kick. You and I together just like old times."

Tony cleared his throat, uncomfortable at the direction in which they were heading and just as uncomfortable at the appeal that road still had. "Claire, things have changed. I'm a minister now."

Her lips quirked upward.

He folded his arms across his chest. "You find that amusing?"

Claire's smile widened. "You might have fooled the others—" she leaned forward and placed her hand flat against his chest "—but I know what you're really like."

Books by Cynthia Rutledge

Love Inspired

CYNTHIA RUTLEDGE

lives in the Midwest and has enjoyed reading romance since her teens. She loves the fact that you can always count on a happy ending.

Writing inspirational romance has been especially gratifying because it allows her to combine her faith in God with her love of romance.

Redeeming Claire is her fourth book for Love Inspired.

Redeeming Claire
Cynthia Rutledge

Published by Steeple Hill Books™

STEEPLE HILL BOOKS

Steeple
Hill™

ISBN 0-373-87158-9

REDEEMING CLAIRE

Copyright © 2001 by Cynthia Rutledge

Visit us at www.steeplehill.com

Printed in U.S.A.

God has not given us a spirit of fear. But he has given us a spirit of power and love and self-control.

—*2 Timothy* 1:7

To Romance authors of the Heartland.
You're a wonderful group of authors
and I've appreciated all your support!

Chapter One

"**C**an't you tell him to shut up?" Claire Waters resisted the urge to cover her ears with her hands. She'd never been overly fond of children, and in front of her the screaming red-faced baby shrieking at the top of his lungs confirmed her good sense.

"If only it could be that easy." Taylor Lanagan laughed and shoved an identical version of the bellowing baby into Claire's arms. "Here, you take this one."

Claire stared in horror at the dark-haired infant. She'd stopped by to get Tony's address and suddenly she'd been appointed Mary Poppins? No way.

Her gaze swept the room, trying to find a place to dispose of the bundle. She pried his chubby fingers from her new silver-blue linen shell, cringing at the wrinkles left behind. The little boy sucked on his pacifier and stared at her with unblinking green eyes fringed with long jet-black lashes.

If she ever did have a baby, she'd rather have one like this. One that knew how to keep his mouth shut. One that didn't cause any trouble.

Not like his brother, a monster that continued to scream even while cradled in his mother's arms. "Claire, I'm sorry. Robbie's usually not this fussy. I think he's cutting teeth."

She wanted to say there was no excuse for bad manners but she doubted Taylor would agree. The woman seemed to be enamored with her twin sons. As was her husband, Nick, the man Claire had once hoped to marry. They were both baby crazy. Despite her father's disappointment, never had Claire been so glad that she and Nick hadn't ended up together.

Tony was definitely more her speed. A fun-loving guy who enjoyed spending money as much as she did.

"The address?" Claire prompted.

"I just got a letter from him. Now where did I put it?" Taylor pulled open a drawer and rifled through a stack of envelopes, bouncing her son on her hip, trying to quiet his wails. "Did I tell you he moved to Iowa?"

"Yes." Claire kept a tight rein on her temper. It wouldn't do to snap at Taylor. Right now the woman was her only link to Tony Karelli. "But knowing the state doesn't do me much good."

"No, this isn't it." Taylor shoved an envelope back into the drawer and grabbed another.

My goodness, how long did it take to find one little address?

"Found it," Taylor said.

Claire could barely hear her above the infant's ear-piercing cry. But she could see Taylor's triumphant expression, and when she waived the envelope in the air, excitement surged through Claire.

Her mind raced ahead, planning her strategy and her wardrobe. Perhaps if she wore one of the eye-catching outfits she'd bought last weekend... Perhaps if she offered to pay Tony twice as much as he was making at his current job... Perhaps if she promised him... She smiled, remembering how Tony's eyes had always gleamed at the mere hint of a little skin. Yes, this was going to work out just fine.

Once her father was pacified, Tony could go back to Hicksville, Iowa, or wherever he'd taken up residence these days, and do whatever it was he'd been doing since he left. And she could go back to doing what she did best—spending her father's money and having a good time.

"Claire." The panic in Taylor's voice caught her attention. "Ryan is spitting up."

The warning came a second too late. Something

warm and foul-smelling dribbled across Claire's chest. Her stomach flip-flopped, and she shrieked in outrage. The baby's grin widened, remnants of his breakfast lingering on his lips.

Taylor sat the fussy Robbie in the playpen and hurriedly took the infant from Claire's arms. It was as if she knew how sorely tempted Claire was to drop the brat right on his padded bottom and wipe that toothless grin from his lips.

"I'm sorry, Claire." Taylor grabbed a cloth diaper from a stack on the desktop. "You know how babies can be."

Claire snatched the snow-white square from Taylor's hand and mopped her chest. Yes, she wanted to tell Taylor, she knew how babies could be, and that's why she didn't have any.

"Of course." Claire bit her tongue and forced a smile. "Could I have that address? I really need to get going."

Taylor scribbled on a sheet of paper and handed it to Claire. "Did I tell you what he's doing now? You'll never believe it."

Claire backed toward the door, the coveted address clutched tightly in her hand. There was no longer a need to extend her visit or even be civil. She'd gotten what she wanted.

"He'd just finished—" The shrill ring of the phone stopped Taylor's words and started both babies crying.

Didn't they ever shut up? Claire wanted to scream. But she didn't have to put up with it now. She moved quickly to the door, opening it in a single jerk. "I'd love to chat but I've got to go."

Taylor opened her mouth, but Claire didn't give her a chance. She gave a jaunty wave, slammed the door behind her and breathed a sigh of relief.

Mission accomplished.

Tony Karelli heaved a relieved sigh. It had been tight, but in the end he'd been able to cram all essential items into the attic area he'd rented until the parsonage could be completed. He'd risen at the crack of dawn, a man with a mission. But now that he had everything unpacked and put away, he was just a hungry man with a growling stomach reminding him that he hadn't eaten since yesterday.

What better way to reward himself for a morning of hard work than by accepting his new landlady's offer of lunch? When he'd rented Darlene Sandy's studio apartment she'd informed him lunch was available from eleven to one every day in the downstairs dining room.

And last night when she'd mentioned that fact once again, she'd added that it would be nice if he stopped down so they could get better acquainted. Her intent was clear. He'd seen the questions in her eyes when he'd rolled into town late last night and read the disappointment on her face when he'd been too tired to stay up and talk. She wanted answers.

A smile creased his lips. Truth be known, he didn't mind answering questions. In fact he was looking forward to getting acquainted. He'd wanted a small town for the very reason many of his classmates didn't. His father had spent years in the military before he went into political service so Tony had moved a lot when he was young. Now, at twenty-eight, he was ready to put down roots. He wanted to get to know everyone in this small Iowa town on a first-name basis. The last thing he wanted was to preach the gospel to a bunch of nameless faces every Sunday.

He'd spent the last two years in the seminary dreaming of this moment. He was eager to get on with his life and start doing God's work. Becoming part of the community in which he would be ministering was a necessary first step.

He headed for the stairs. The door clicked shut behind him and locked automatically. He smiled, remembering how Mrs. Sandy had been almost apologetic about the need to lock the doors. It was necessary, she explained, because of all the out-of-town people who stayed in the house.

It was funny. He'd grown up in cities where you'd never consider *not* locking your doors. In fact most of the homes he'd lived in had security systems that rivaled those at Fort Knox. But Mrs. Sandy had felt she had to explain why they locked the doors. It was another indication that he'd made the right choice in coming to Millville.

Tony headed down the two flights to the main floor. The smell of fresh baked bread grew stronger with each step. He paused at the first landing and glanced at his watch. Ten minutes and lunch would be over. He increased his speed.

As his feet hit the hardwood floor of the foyer, he caught a glimpse of himself in the beveled mirror on the opposite wall and skidded to a stop. His hand rose to rub the dark stubble on his cheeks, and he stifled a curse. He'd been so busy unpacking he'd forgotten to shave. And that wasn't all. He glanced at the well-worn jeans and Denver Bronco's T-shirt he pulled on this morning. They'd been fine for working in his apartment, but he knew his mother would have had a fit if he'd showed up at *her* table in such casual attire. But his mother was a Washington socialite, and Mrs. Sandy was—well, Mrs. Sandy.

A mouthwatering aroma mingled with the smell of the bread, and his stomach growled again, more insistently this time. If he took time to change, he'd miss lunch. He headed toward the dining room.

Sunlight streamed in through a huge window overlooking the spacious front yard. The leaded glass at the top scattered rainbows of light throughout the tastefully appointed room. His heart sank as he realized the dining room was empty.

Disappointment coursed through his veins. A day late and a dollar short.

The story of my life.

Not anymore, he reminded himself. Not since he'd put his life in God's hands.

The door to the kitchen burst open, and Tony shifted his gaze. A short, plump woman with tightly permed hair and a friendly face plowed through the doorway. She stopped abruptly and her eyes widened. "Pastor Karelli. I didn't know you were here."

"I just came down for lunch." Tony smiled ruefully and gestured to the empty table. "But I guess I'm a little too late."

"Nonsense." Mrs. Sandy's smile widened. "April—that's my daughter—and I were just sitting down to eat in the kitchen. We'd love to have you join us."

"I wouldn't want to intrude."

"How can you intrude?" The woman chuckled. "We're all living under the same roof, so you're family now. C'mon, the soup is getting cold."

The tension that had tightened his neck into knots eased. He'd never been as comfortable with strangers as he appeared. He hoped it wouldn't be long until he felt as if they were family. He smiled and followed her into the kitchen.

A pretty blonde with enormous blue eyes sat at the table. She straightened in her chair the moment Tony walked through the door.

"Pastor Karelli, this is my daughter April."

Tony stared, baffled. "I thought you said your daughter was in high school?"

A pleased expression blanketed April's face, and she laughed, a sultry purr so far removed from a girlish giggle as to not even be comparable. She'd taken the hand he'd extended and held it, making no effort to let go. Her manicured nails were long and a vibrant shade of pink. For an instant an image of Claire Waters flashed. This girl had the same blatant sensuality that Claire had always projected, only April was a small-town version. "I may not look seventeen, but then you don't look like a pastor, either."

"We all have our cross to bear." Tony smiled politely and pulled back his hand. He took a seat at the table opposite April.

Mrs. Sandy chuckled and filled his bowl with a noodle and vegetable concoction that smelled delicious before shifting her gaze to her daughter. "April, be sure and get those beds made before you leave for the video store."

April ignored her mother; her gaze focused on Tony. "I could call in sick at the store. I'd be glad to show you around town."

He didn't even have to come up with an excuse.

Mrs. Sandy leveled a glinting gaze at her daughter. "You begged me to let you take that job. And I agreed even though it's leaving me shorthanded here. Don't you even think about not going in."

A petulant look crossed the girl's face, and in that moment Tony caught a glimpse of the teenager behind the carefully applied makeup.

"I'm not hungry after all." April pushed back her chair with a clatter and stood, carefully avoiding her mother's gaze. She smiled at Tony. "Maybe another time."

"Sure," he said.

Mrs. Sandy filled her own bowl with soup and took the seat vacated by her daughter. She shook her head in disgust. "Teenagers."

Tony cut a slice of the homemade bread sitting in the middle of the table and didn't comment.

"Were you like that as a teenager, Pastor? Always on the go with your friends? In such a hurry to grow up?"

The memories flooded back. He'd been a geek as a teen. With his braces, glasses, acne and a few extra pounds, he'd been lucky to have any friends, much less any place to go. His only goal had been to fit in. If he hadn't had Taylor...

He pushed the thought aside. She was married now, happily married, with two little boys.

"Pastor?"

Tony realized with a start that the question

hadn't been rhetorical. The woman actually expected an answer. "Not really."

The woman's look was clearly disbelieving, but he'd spoken the truth. His nights had been filled with books, video games and television. Classic nerd activities.

"Did you and your fiancée meet in high school or college?"

For a second he'd sworn she'd said fiancée. He took a sip of his cola. Maybe he wasn't as awake as he thought. "When I was in high school I had friends that were girls, but nothing serious. We were more good friends rather than boyfriend, girlfriend."

Mrs. Sandy nodded approvingly. "That's what I try to tell April. She's got plenty of time to get serious when she's older."

"That's true." He took another bit of the thick oat bread.

"How long then have you and your fiancée known each other?"

Tony choked on the bread. He reached for the cola. This time he was sure he hadn't misheard. The woman had definitely said fiancée.

"Mrs. Sandy." He cleared his throat and paused. He didn't want to embarrass the poor woman, but he had to clear up her obvious mistake. She'd been on the selection committee, and she must have gotten him mixed up with Josh Turner,

the other finalist for the position. Josh and his fiancée, Andrea, were the ones planning on being
married in July. "I'm not—"

The phone rang, and she picked it up immediately. "Yes, he's here."

She held her hand over the receiver and whispered. "It's Harold Clarke."

Harold was an elder and the head of the church
council. He'd been the one who'd made the final
decision on which candidate got the call.

"No, his fiancée isn't here yet." She smiled at
Tony.

A band tightened around his chest.

"I'm not sure if she's coming down before the
wedding or not. We haven't gotten that far. Sure,
I'll be here all day. Stop over anytime."

She hung up the phone and turned her attention
to Tony. "Now where were we?"

He answered her question with one of his own,
stalling for time. "Is Mr. Clarke stopping by?"

"He said he'd try. I know he wants to be one
of the first to welcome you to town. But the bank
keeps him pretty busy this time of year. And then
he's got those three teenagers who are into everything." She poured herself a cup of coffee and held
up the pot. He shook his head.

"I shouldn't probably tell you this, but family
is really important to Harold. The fact that you
were getting married really swayed his vote in your

favor. The other man I'm sure would have been fine, but Harold was hesitant, what with him being single and all.''

Tony stifled a groan. They *had* gotten him confused with Josh. What was he going to do now? He'd given up his apartment in DC and spent the last of his money to move halfway across the country. Would he even have a job once they discovered their mistake?

The truth needed to come out. But maybe he should speak with Mr. Clarke first, plead his case. Tony knew he could do a good job if given the chance.

"I remember what we were talking about." Mrs. Sandy leaned forward, her eyes gleaming. "We were talking about your fiancée. Andrea, isn't it?"

He stared unblinking, his mind racing. He was way over his head and sinking fast.

Dear God, help me.

The doorbell rang, and Mrs. Sandy looked up, startled. Tony heaved a relieved sigh. Once again he'd been saved by the bell.

"Harold must have come right over." Mrs. Sandy shoved back her chair and stood. She took off her apron, draping it across the back of the chair.

The doorbell rang again.

She fluffed her curls with the tips of her fingers before heading for the front door.

Tony rose, feeling like a condemned prisoner on his way to the gas chamber. Condemned prisoner? No way. He forced himself to remember that he might think this is where he was meant to be but God might have other plans. Whatever happened would be His will.

Squaring his shoulders, Tony headed to the front door. He'd meet this challenge head-on. After all, he hadn't done anything wrong.

He slowed as he rounded the corner leading to the front foyer. It sounded almost as if Mrs. Sandy was speaking to a woman. The husky voice of the visitor was naggingly familiar. But how could that be?

"Yes, he's here. In fact we're just having lunch. We'd love for you to join us." Mrs. Sandy opened the door wider just as Tony stepped into view.

He stopped short, unable to believe his eyes. Sanding there with a bag in each hand and a Cheshire cat smile plastered across her face was the one woman he'd thought he'd never see again.

Chapter Two

"**D**arling, aren't you going to give me a kiss?"

Tony could only stare and wonder if Claire Waters was a vision that his sleep-deprived brain had conjured up to torment him. She looked beautiful. Stunning, actually. Her long black hair was pulled back in a simple twist, and her pale yellow dress highlighted her dark tan.

She didn't wait for his answer. Claire brushed past Mrs. Sandy and wrapped her arms around his neck. "You have to know how much I've missed you."

The light provocative scent of her perfume teased his nostrils, and almost of their own volition his hands moved to her waist.

"I've missed you, too." It was his voice but it was as if someone else had spoken the words.

She smiled and tilted her face upward. He lowered his mouth obligingly. Her lips were warm and sweet, and he lost himself in the kiss. It had indeed been too long.

"Oh, my." Mrs. Sandy tittered, and Tony jerked back.

"What do we have here?"

His heart plummeted at the sound of the deep baritone resonating from the open doorway. Tony slowly turned his head and met Harold Clarke's amused gaze.

"Mr. Clarke." Tony disentangled himself from Claire's arms. He extended one hand and resisted the urge to wipe her lipstick from his mouth with the back of the other. "What a surprise."

Mrs. Sandy laughed. "I told you Harold was going to stop by."

"That's right." Tony flashed a smile. "You did."

"Let's cut the guy some slack, Darlene." Harold shook Tony's hand and slanted a sideways glance at Claire. "It isn't every day a man is reunited with his fiancée."

Claire raised one dark brow but didn't deny the man's mistaken impression. She merely brushed a strand of hair that had pulled loose in their embrace away from her face and shifted her gaze to Tony.

He had to admire her composure. She was cool and collected while he stood on the edge of blurting out a confession. Subterfuge had never been his strength.

"Mr. Clarke." Tony hesitated, raking his fingers through his hair. This wasn't the way he'd wanted to discuss the mistake they'd made, but now it seemed he didn't have a choice.

"Darling." Claire grasped his arm, her nails digging into his skin. "I've been traveling since early this morning. I'm exhausted and I'd really like to sit down."

"Of course, my dear." Mrs. Sandy picked up Claire's suitcase. "Forgive my poor manners. Let's go into the parlor and I'll get us some iced tea."

The thought of prolonging this agony a moment longer was unbearable. "Wait. I need to explain—"

"I said don't worry about it." Harold's tone broached no argument. "I'm glad to see that you and your fiancée have such a close and loving relationship."

"Tony is a very affectionate guy." The twinkle in Claire's eyes told Tony she might not understand what was going on, but she'd decided to have some fun with it. His unease skyrocketed.

"Sweetheart, stop." He smiled through gritted teeth and shot her a warning glance. All he needed was for her to make a bad situation worse.

Her smile widened. His irritation seemed to please her. An icy chill traveled up Tony's spine.

He knew all too well what this woman was capable of doing. Her warm greeting only moments before was no guarantee she'd treat him kindly.

"Everybody, just take a seat. I'll be back in a jiffy." Mrs. Sandy hurried into the kitchen.

Mr. Clarke's gaze followed her out of the room before shifting to Claire, who'd settled on the sofa next to Tony. "I don't believe we've been properly introduced." He extended his hand. "I'm Harold Clarke."

"Mr. Clarke is an elder and head of the church council." Tony could only hope she understood the significance of the information he'd just imparted. If she didn't he could be sunk deeper than the *Titanic* in a matter of minutes.

"And I know who you are," Harold said teasingly. "We heard all about the lovely Andrea when Tony interviewed for the position."

"My name is Claire," she said sweetly.

"Andrea Claire," Tony said instantly, covering her hand with his and squeezing it. Hard. "Andrea Claire Waters."

"That's right." Her laugh sounded forced to Tony, but Harold didn't seem to find anything amiss. Especially when she leaned forward and batted her long dark lashes, her painted lips tilting upward. "Harold—you don't mind if I call you Harold, do you?"

"Of course not."

"And you must call me Claire."

Tony watched in amazement while Claire went to work. The woman had flirting down to an art form. The guy never knew what hit him. By the time Mrs. Sandy returned with a tray filled with tea and a plate of cookies, the two were laughing like old friends.

"Now, Harold, what is it that you do for a living?" Claire took a glass from Mrs. Sandy without even glancing up or uttering a word of thanks.

"I'm a banker."

"A banker?" Claire raised a brow.

"Actually I own the bank," the man said proudly. "As well as several others in nearby towns."

"I knew you were a businessman the moment I saw you." Claire almost purred the words.

If Tony didn't know better, he'd think she was really interested in the guy. But he knew Harold was too old to hold her interest and not nearly rich enough to suit her tastes.

"What gave it away?"

Her voice lowered to a sultry whisper. "You have the look. The clothes, the hair, the smell—" she wrinkled her nose "—of success."

"Is that right?" Despite the amused gleam in Harold's eyes, Tony could see Claire had pulled the poor sap into her web.

"Absolutely." She smiled widely, her teeth incredibly straight and white.

"I'll get us some more napkins." Mrs. Sandy stood abruptly and left the room.

Claire and Harold paid no attention. Tony stared thoughtfully at the woman's stiffened spine. For a moment he could have sworn she was jealous.

"My father is a businessman, very successful. You have that same look," Claire said.

Harold cleared his throat. "What is it your father does?"

Claire crossed one leg, her short skirt giving Tony and Harold ample view of her long, shapely legs. "He used to own a data warehousing operation. He sold that business several years ago. Now?" She paused and her brow furrowed. "He's pursuing a business venture with one of his friends."

Mrs. Sandy returned, but without the napkins. Her hair looked as if it had been combed and her lipstick freshly applied.

His landlady took the chair next to Tony and smiled sweetly at Claire. "Your father and Harold must be about the same age. They'd probably have a lot in common."

Tony hid a grin behind his hand.

Claire stared at Mrs. Sandy for a moment as if trying to place who she was. "Actually Daddy is a lot older than Harold and not nearly as handsome.''

"Harold has three teenagers at home," Mrs. Sandy said.

"I'm sorry," Claire said. "How awful for you."

A startled expression crossed the man's face. "They're good kids. Of course it's hard being a single parent."

"Does your ex live in town?"

"My wife died five years ago," Harold said, a flash of pain skittering across his face.

"How horrible," Claire said, donning an expression of sympathy. "But I bet a handsome guy like you has the women beating down his door."

Tony stifled a groan.

"Claire, was your father ever disappointed that your fiancé didn't choose to join him in his business?"

Score one for Mrs. Sandy. She'd pulled Claire's attention away from Harold and reminded her she had a fiancé all in one breath.

Claire's gaze swept the woman up and down. "Daddy's still hoping he'll be able to convince Tony that enterprise software is where it's at."

Tony choked on his tea.

"Are you saying he doesn't feel that being a minister is a worthy calling?" Mrs. Sandy's eyes narrowed. "And it almost sounds as if you agree with him."

Claire slanted Tony a quick glance. He could read the confusion in her eyes.

"Claire was actually the one that encouraged me to go into the ministry," Tony said quickly.

"Really?" The approval in Harold's eyes prompted Tony to continue.

"That's right." He smiled at Claire. "I remember it vividly. We were having coffee in Cedar Ridge, Claire's hometown, discussing an upcoming wedding of some friends, and the more we talked, the clearer it became that the ministry was where I belonged."

Harold shifted his attention to Claire. "So you don't have any qualms about being a minister's wife?"

"You want me to be honest?" Claire took a sip of her iced tea, her face suddenly serious.

Tony's hand tightened around his glass, and he forced himself to breathe.

Harold leaned forward in his chair. "Of course I do."

"Like I told my father before I left town, there's no place I'd rather be than at Tony's side." She flashed a bright smile. "And the fact that he's in the ministry... well, it's just an added plus."

"Can I be honest?" Tony paced the floor of the deserted church, his voice mimicking hers. "Mind telling me what was that all about?"

He'd brought her to the church to explain everything. They needed a place to talk where they couldn't be overheard. When Harold had held out the keys to the church, Tony had jumped at the chance to get Claire out of there.

"I was jerking your chain." Claire laughed. "Actually it was fun. I might do it again."

"Don't you realize what's at stake here?"

Claire shot him a narrowed, glinting gaze. "Not really. Ask me if I care." She lifted her shoulders in a slight shrug. "Not really."

Tony took a deep breath and bit back the angry words that sprang from the depth of his frustration. He'd hoped everything would go right when he'd received this call.

"I can't believe you're a minister." Her gaze slid up and down his muscular form. "What a waste."

He bit back the urge to tell her he was a minister, not a priest. Only the thought of how she'd take it held him back. "We need to talk."

"You mean straighten out our stories?" She smiled impishly. "Actually I think it's kind of fun to wing it."

Maybe fun for you, he thought. You don't have anything to lose. For him, it had been torture, pure and simple.

"On the other hand." She leaned back against the cabinet containing the hymnals and stared thoughtfully. "Maybe I *should* let you explain. Okay, lay it on me. What's the scoop?"

"It's sort of complicated." He knew he was stalling but he needed to figure out a way to explain the mess he'd gotten himself into that made some kind of sense. "Why don't you go first? Tell me how you found me and what brings you to Millville."

"Taylor gave me your address," she said.

He wished it was Taylor standing in front of him now, instead of Claire. He could count on his old friend to help him. He wasn't so sure of Claire. "How is she?"

Claire gave a careless shrug. "She doesn't look like a blimp any more, if that's what you want to know."

"Taylor's always been thin."

"Ha," Claire said. "You should have seen her six months ago."

"You mean before she had the twins?"

"I don't see how Nick could bear to look at her." Claire shuddered. "Love must truly be blind."

At one time, he'd wished it could be him marrying Taylor. But he realized now it wasn't part of God's plan. Still, when he did marry, he hoped it would be to a woman like her. "She sent me pictures of the boys. Cute kids."

"They're okay, I guess," Claire said grudgingly. "But they're monsters. Especially that Rob-bie. That kid screams continually. No wonder some women leave their kids. You'd have to have nerves of steel to put up with that.

"Mothers don't leave their children."

"Some do," Claire insisted. A strange expression crossed her face, but it was gone in an instant.

"I'm sure Taylor can handle it." Tony laughed. "But you still haven't told me what brought you here."

"You owe me a favor, and I'm here to collect."

"Favor? How do you figure?"

"Let's sit down somewhere and I'll remind you of what you so conveniently seem to have forgotten." She slipped one shoe off and rubbed her foot. "I bought these heels in New York a couple of weeks ago, and they're killing my feet."

"My new office should be down this hall some-where."

She slid her pump on, and Tony followed her down a shiny aisle that gleamed as if it had been freshly waxed. In no time at all they stood in front of a door with the word Pastor in raised gilt letters.

Tony paused, unprepared for the emotion well-ing up from deep inside. He'd prayed for this day, and now it was here. He'd finally be able to serve God to his fullest ability.

Thank You.

"What are we waiting for?" Claire spoke in her usual blunt manner. "An invitation?"

Tony had to chuckle. Claire never changed. He turned the knob and ushered her in.

Her nose wrinkled. "It smells funny in here."

"I think it's just from being shut up." Tony raised the blinds and cracked open the window. Sunlight flooded the room.

He glanced around. The dark wood paneling was reminiscent of an earlier era, but the burgundy leather chairs were in good shape, and a new computer sat on the desktop.

"This place definitely needs professional help." Claire's gaze shifted to the side counter adorned by an oversize bouquet of silk flowers in a burgundy vase. A look of horror crossed her face. "Good Lord."

"Claire," Tony warned.

"Don't tell me you actually like those hideous things." Her eyes widened in melodramatic shock. "Next thing I know you'll have those magnetic goldfish on your desk."

"Actually I was thinking of getting a couple of them." He made sure he kept a straight face. Dangerous as it could be, he enjoyed teasing her. "One for me and one for you."

"Do that and you'll get that cheap plastic bowl smashed over your thick head."

He laughed.

"You think I'm kidding."

"No, but I am." He couldn't keep from grinning. "But I'm totally serious when I say I'd like it if you could stay awhile."

"I might," she said. "At least until Daddy calms down."

"What's got your father upset?"

"You know how unreasonable he can be," she said, skirting the question. "We needed some time apart. So here I am."

"I haven't seen you in two years."

"I know." Claire winked. "It's been way too long."

He stared. She was up to something. The question was—what?

"Darling, don't look so suspicious." Her voice turned low and sultry. She reminded him of a cat closing in on its prey. "It'll be a kick. You and I together just like old times."

Tony cleared his throat, uncomfortable at the direction in which they were heading and just as uncomfortable at the appeal that road still had. "Claire, things have changed. I'm a minister now."

Her lips quirked upward.

He folded his arms across his chest. "You find that amusing?"

Claire's smile widened. "You might have fooled the others—" she leaned forward and placed her hand flat against his chest "—but I know what you're really like."

"You don't know anything about me." He jerked back, his skin hot beneath her touch. "You never even tried to get to know me. You just wanted to use me to break up Nick and Taylor."

She stilled and stared for a long moment. "Well, I guess that makes us even, doesn't it?"

"Even?"

"Oh, please, Tony. I may be a lot of things but I'm not a fool." Her eyes narrowed. "For some reason you want everyone to think I'm your fiancée. That's okay with me. But if you're going to use me for your own purposes, I need to know the game plan before..."

"Before?" he prompted, a knot forming in the pit of his stomach.

"Before I decide what it's going to cost you."

Chapter Three

"**M**arilyn Marshall, our last minister's wife, led a Wednesday morning Bible study. I know we've all missed it." Mrs. Sandy peered at Claire over the top of her cup. "Would you be interested in starting that up again?"

Claire resisted the urge to look at her watch. They'd barely returned from the church when Harold had whisked Tony away, leaving her to deal with Mrs. Sandy. So far the woman hadn't been too bad, but Claire sensed that was about to change.

"Perhaps." Claire feigned an interested smile. "But not right away. I'd like to get settled first."

"I completely understand." Mrs. Sandy patted her hand. "Those wedding plans will be keeping you busy."

Claire took another sip of her fruit juice and wished for something a little stronger. "Uh-huh."

"What day are you getting married?" The landlady took her third brownie from the plate and tilted her head. "I know it's in July sometime."

Claire smiled, keeping her expression noncommittal. The more she thought, the more sure she was that she and Tony never discussed a date.

Absently she took a bite of the brownie Mrs. Sandy had shoved before her. The chocolate sweetness melted against her tongue.

Claire dropped the rest of the gooey concoction to the plate. She needed to stop this mindless eating or she'd end up leaving town with a suitcase full of clothes that wouldn't fit.

"Claire?"

She wiped her mouth with a napkin and swallowed hard. "Yes?"

"What day are you getting married?" Mrs. Sandy asked again. "July..."

"Fourth." The date popped out before she could stop it. When she'd been a little girl Independence Day had been her favorite holiday. Her mother had loved the fireworks and all the parades. She shoved the memories aside.

"You're getting married on the Fourth of July?" The woman's tone was clearly disbelieving.

It was almost worth the gaffe, Claire decided, to see Mrs. Sandy try to conceal her shock. Claire gave a little shrug. "Tony picked the day. Personally I thought it was a little strange."

"What's strange?"

A familiar deep voice sounded from the doorway, and Claire's heart skipped a beat. She took another sip of the too tart orange juice.

"That we're getting married on the Fourth of July." She lifted her gaze and met his. "I told Mrs. Sandy that I thought it was strange but that you'd insisted."

To his credit, his smile appeared genuine. But she noticed he didn't answer right away. He slipped behind her, and his hand settled on her shoulder. Obviously a ploy to bide time.

"I know it's unusual." Tony chuckled. "But I've always called Claire my little firecracker, so it seemed fitting."

He'd taken the ball she'd tossed him and scored a touchdown. Her respect for him inched upward. She'd always admired a man who could think on his feet, especially a handsome one. Her gaze met his, and they shared a smile.

A sad expression flitted across Mrs. Sandy's face. "John used to call me pumpkin."

Pumpkin?

Fat, round, orange. Claire bit her lip to keep from laughing out loud. The word fit the woman.

"So I take it you were married on Halloween?"

"Claire." Tony's low voice was filled with reproach.

"What?" She straightened in her chair, and her jaw tightened. "You call me your firecracker and we're getting married on the Fourth." The words rolled awkwardly from her lips. "He called her his pumpkin—"

"Stop it, you two." Mrs. Sandy laughed. "I'm not offended at all. John and I were married in October, so I guess I was sort of a harvest bride."

Claire shot Tony a smug grin. "Where is your husband? Will I meet him later?"

It wouldn't be long before she'd have John Sandy wrapped around her finger, like she had Harold Clarke. She'd always liked men more than women.

The woman hesitated. "John was killed last year in an explosion at the co-op."

It was obvious she'd loved the man very much. Claire's gaze shifted to Tony, and she eyed him speculatively. Would she ever love someone that much? It hardly seemed likely. "Was he killed instantly?"

Mrs. Sandy's eyes widened in surprise. It was almost as if no one had asked her that question before. "Why, yes, he was."

Tony's fingers dug deep into her shoulder. "Knowing he died in the faith must have been a comfort."

"John is with God now. I have no doubt." The woman dabbed at her eyes with the tip of her napkin. "But knowing he didn't suffer was also a comfort."

Mrs. Sandy blinked several times and took a deep breath. "Would you like a brownie, Pastor?"

Claire studied the woman thoughtfully. Darlene Sandy did possess a certain amount of class. For a pumpkin.

Tony pulled out a dining room chair and sat down next to Claire. "It's tempting, but I think I'll pass. Harold and I stopped at the Gas 'N' Go when he was showing me around town and I picked up a doughnut."

A pastry from a gas station? What would be next? Tony in a seed cap talking about hogs? Claire cringed at the thought. Thank goodness she'd be long gone before that happened.

"I assume Harold talked to you about the barbecue tomorrow night," Mrs. Sandy said.

"It sounds great." Tony nodded. "But you didn't have to go to all that trouble for me."

"We're happy to do it." The color had returned to Mrs. Sandy's cheeks, and the haunted look had left her eye. "The community can't wait to meet the new pastor. And his fiancée," she added.

Claire knew what that meant. They couldn't wait to scrutinize the new minister and spend the rest of the night talking about him...and her. Claire certainly wouldn't fault them. If the situations were reversed, she'd be doing the exact same thing.

Her thoughts shifted to her suitcase, still sitting unopened in the hall. She tried to remember what she'd packed and if she had anything suitable for a barbecue.

If not, Des Moines would be the closest city for shopping. If you could call Des Moines a city. Still, she should be able to find *something* there. Especially with the help of Daddy's platinum credit card.

"I'm going to unpack." Claire pushed back her chair and stood. She'd socialized long enough. "Maybe take a nap."

Tony nodded and rose slowly. "Are you sure you want to go to the motel already?"

"Motel?" Claire frowned. "What in the world are you talking about?"

"You said you wanted to get settled in."

Surely, he didn't think she'd be staying at the motel. She'd caught a glimpse of the dump on the way into town. A typical mom-and-pop operation whose decor hadn't been updated since the sixties. "Not at the Shabby Inn."

"It's the Shady Inn," Mrs. Sandy corrected.

"Whatever." Claire shrugged. "The point is I wouldn't be caught dead in a place like that."

"Where are you going to stay then?"

"Why, sweetheart." She flashed Tony a bright

smile and gave him a wink. "I thought I'd stay here with you."

Mrs. Sandy choked on her coffee.

Tony blanched.

Claire laughed. "Not *with* you, silly. After all, we're not married yet."

She caught the approval in Mrs. Sandy's eyes and the relief in Tony's face. Her gaze lingered appreciatively on the elegant Victorian furnishings. "I meant I'll rent one of the rooms in this house. Actually, I'll take your very best room."

"I'm sorry, Claire." Regret shown on the round face. "But I only have three guest rooms, and they're booked solid through August."

"You must have something." Claire stared. Surely the woman wasn't serious. What was she to do? She wanted to stay here. Claire forced herself to calm down and think how her father would handle such a situation. "I'll pay you twice as much as you normally get."

"I couldn't." Mrs. Sandy shook her head. "Some of these people have had reservations for months."

Never take no for an answer.

"But there's got to be a way." Claire shot the woman her best sugarcoated smile.

"I do have the maid's quarters, but light housekeeping goes along with that space."

Claire smiled in satisfaction. Listening to her father rant and rave all these years had been worth it, after all. "I'll take the room. You can find someone else for the housekeeping."

Not for one moment would she even consider doing manual labor. Picking up her clothes from the floor before the cleaning lady came was bad enough. Claire smiled appreciatively at her recently manicured nails and her soft-as-silk hands. Some people were made for physical work. Some weren't.

"I'm sorry, but that won't do." Mrs. Sandy shook her head.

"Why wouldn't it?" Claire kept her voice calm, trying to still her rising panic.

"I really need some live-in help. Especially since April took that job at the video store."

"April?"

"April is Mrs. Sandy's daughter, Claire," Tony said.

Claire disliked her already. If the girl would help her mother instead of wasting her time shoving videos across a counter for minimum wage, that room would be available.

"She's a senior in high school," Tony added. "And a beautiful girl."

All the more reason to hate her.

Claire slanted a sideways glance at Mrs. Sandy. A beautiful girl?

Tony was either being incredibly kind, or the girl took after her father.

Claire paused, beyond caring what Mrs. Sandy's daughter looked like or why she'd taken some job and left her mother in the lurch. It had been a long day, and Claire's head throbbed. She desperately needed a long soak in a tub, a facial and a massage. But she doubted that most people in this tiny bump-in-the-road town even knew what a day spa was, much less had one. That left the motel to provide the tub and Tony for the massage. The facial would have to wait until another time.

"I don't mean to be rude, but I'd really like to freshen up." It took all her inner strength to continue and utter the foreign word. "Do you think the...motel...will have an empty room?"

"They always have space," Mrs. Sandy said promptly.

Claire knew the woman was trying to be reassuring, but her words had the opposite effect. After all, what kind of place always had rooms? The suites of the establishments she frequented with her father were always booked well in advance. But then again, they'd never considered a...motel.

"Okay." Claire forced a smile. "Tony can drive me."

She didn't even bother to phrase it as a question. Of course, he would want to take her. "Then we can go out to dinner and to a movie."

Tony shifted uncomfortably. "Mrs. Sandy is having the church council members and their spouses over tonight."

Claire raised a brow.

"It's sort of a meet-the-pastor kind of get-together."

"But this is my first night here."

"Sweetheart, we didn't know you were coming." Tony smiled, but Claire could hear the hint of reproach in his voice.

"What am I supposed to do all night?" Irritation surged through her. There was no way she was going to sit alone in that motel room all night.

"Actually you're invited, too, my dear." Mrs. Sandy cast an anxious glance from Tony to Claire. "You're part of the team."

Of course she was. Everybody knew if a minister had a wife the congregation was doubly blessed, two workers for the price of one. Claire was tempted to say as much but she held her tongue. In large part due to the pleading look in Tony's brown eyes.

"I suppose I could make an appearance." Claire's thoughts returned to the limited wardrobe she'd packed. "What will everyone be wearing?"

If she'd known she'd have all these functions to attend, she would have brought a whole trunk load of clothes. Still, perhaps her clingy black silk cocktail dress might work in a pinch.

"I don't think anybody will wear jeans," Mrs. Sandy said, her expression thoughtful.

Jeans? Startled, Claire jerked her head up. She would never have considered jeans an option.

"Although some of the women might wear a denim jumper," Mrs. Sandy added.

Claire widened her eyes. Visions of overweight women in voluminous jumpers danced in her head. Her lips twitched.

"It's just a little get-together, Claire." As if he could read her mind, Tony squeezed her hand, a warning glint in his eyes. "Everyone will be dressed casually. Why don't you wear that cute little red dress of yours? The one made out of that stretchy material."

At first she couldn't figure out what he was talking about. Then she remembered. It hadn't been red, but rather brick. And the stretchy fabric had been a rayon, polyester and spandex blend.

When Tony had spent the summer in Cedar Ridge, he'd loved that dress.

"How sweet that you remembered." Claire patted his hand. "Unfortunately that was forever ago, and even if I still had it, I wouldn't have a clue where it could be."

"Mom, Matt don't want—"

Claire shifted her gaze to the intruder with the horrid English. A blond-haired teenage girl stood in the doorway, a slightly older young man behind her.

"April, I'm glad you're home." Mrs. Sandy rose and motioned the two into the dining room. "Come in and meet Pastor Karelli's fiancée."

"You're engaged?" The girl's startled gaze shifted from Tony to Claire.

That's right, honey. He's mine.

"I'm Claire Waters." Claire smiled sweetly but couldn't resist adding, "Tony's fiancée."

"We knew she would eventually be moving to Millville." Mrs. Sandy rattled on. "We just didn't know it would be this soon."

"Claire, this is April, Mrs. Sandy's daughter. And her friend…" Tony turned to the boy.

"Matt." His gaze dropped from Claire's eyes down to the rest of her. "Coukle."

"What an interesting last name. Cuckoo." Claire's lips tilted upward in an amused smile. "Matt Cuckoo. Any relation to the clock?"

"It's Coukle," he snapped. A hint of red stole up his neck, his youthful arrogance somehow diminished by a single word.

"Sorry." Claire smiled, not sorry at all. The boy deserved to be taken down a peg or two. She knew his type. He was nothing more than a big fish in a small pond. In a large city he would have been one most women would have tossed back in an instant.

But April was young and naive. Claire almost felt sorry for her.

"Claire, we'd better get you checked in." Tony pushed back his chair and stood.

"Checked in?" April's gaze shifted to her mother. "Isn't she staying here?"

"All our rooms are full, April. You know that," Mrs. Sandy said. "Claire's going to be staying at the Shady Inn."

"That dump?" April hooted. "Hey, good luck to you."

"I don't need luck." Despite her misgivings, Claire refused to give the girl any measure of satisfaction. "If the place is unsuitable I won't be staying there."

She and Tony hurried through their goodbyes, promising to return at seven for the barbecue.

They made it all the way to the car before Tony spoke. "What did you mean about not staying at the Shady Inn?"

"Just what I said." She turned to face him and lifted her chin.

"But where will you go?"

"I might change my mind and stay with you." His apartment was beautiful, and there was more than enough room for her. The sofa in the living room even folded out into a bed.

"Think how that would look."

"Worried about your reputation, *Pastor?*"

"No," he said softly, his hand rising to push a strand of her hair from her face, his lips softly brushing her cheek. "I'm worried about yours."

She stared, and despite herself, a warm glow of satisfaction swept through her. He hadn't disappointed her. Not at all.

Chapter Four

Tony wheeled the Jeep into the Shady Inn's parking lot and pulled to a stop in front of the entrance. Shivers of dread coursed up Claire's spine. The place looked even worse up close. Paint hung in loose strips off the hardboard siding, and yellow dandelions sprung up here and there in the gravel-covered parking lot.

There was only one other vehicle in the lot, an orange station wagon with a Go Hawkeyes bumper sticker in the back window.

"Looks like they need to run a weekend special," Claire joked, trying unsuccessfully to smother her sense of foreboding.

Tony reached over and squeezed her hand. "I know it's not a Hilton, but I'm sure it'll be fine."

It was all Claire could do not to roll her eyes.

Tony was the eternal optimist. She preferred to be realistic. The instant they drove up she knew everything was not going to be fine. She stared through the windshield at her new home away from home, and her heart sank to the tips of her alligator shoes.

With a heavy sigh of resignation, Claire slowly opened the car door and stepped out.

"It looks better up close," Tony said.

Startled, she glanced from the handmade welcome sign hanging crookedly from a thumbtack in the door to the gingham curtains on the window. Had Tony lost his mind? Or better yet, his eyesight?

"Yeah, it's definitely got that Martha Stewart touch."

Her sarcasm seemed lost on him. He smiled absently, pushed open the door and motioned Claire inside.

She took a deep breath, straightened her shoulders and entered the lobby feeling like a prisoner walking into a cell block.

"Welcome." A heavyset man in his mid-fifties smiled broadly from behind the counter. "Need a room tonight?"

No, we just stopped by to say hello.

"Good afternoon." Claire forced herself to maintain a civil tone. It wouldn't do to alienate the natives. Plus she needed to consider that there were probably many people—her gaze settled on a Hawaiian hula doll in the windowsill—make that at least a few people who wouldn't mind staying here. "I'll take your best room."

"I'm afraid all of our rooms are the same—" the man chuckled "—'cept of course you get your choice of two doubles or a king."

Claire could only stare. At the very least she'd hoped they'd have *one* suite.

"We'll take one with a king," Tony said.

"Good choice." The desk clerk smiled and winked. "Me and the missus used to sleep on a double. Those beds are okay, but you're practically on top of each other." His gaze settled on Claire. "Not that that's all bad, mind you."

"Miss Waters will be the only one staying here." A silken thread of warning ran through Tony's voice, but his smile softened the words and he extended his hand in greeting. "I'm Pastor Karelli. I'm the new minister at Grace Community over on Elm."

"Floyd Peeks. I'm the owner. Pleased to meet you." The man shook Tony's hand before his gaze once again shifted to Claire.

"And this is Claire Waters," Tony said. "My fiancée."

"You sure are a pretty little thing," Floyd said, his smile widening.

Claire raised a brow. Tony's hand tightened on her arm.

"Thank you." She forced a smile. "Would it be possible for you to show me the room? I'd like to see it before I commit to anything."

"Shore thing." Floyd grabbed a set of keys hanging from a nail and hollered, "Honey, watch the front. I'll be gone for a few minutes."

A feminine voice sounded from the back, barely perceptible over a blaring television. Floyd nodded and led them outside without a backward glance.

In a matter of minutes Claire's hopes for a simple but elegant room were dashed by a heavy dose of reality.

The room was simple, all right. If she'd been feeling particularly kind, she'd have called it quaint. But it was about as far from elegant as you could get. A slightly musty odor permeated the interior, and Claire noticed both the bathroom sink and the tub had large rust stains around the drain.

Claire followed Mr. Peeks back to the office, Tony's arm resting companionably around her shoulders. She tried to still her unease by telling herself this was only temporary. She'd just be staying until Daddy calmed down. If only she knew how long that would take.

When she'd taken his new Mercedes convertible in high school without permission and promptly totaled it, things had been back to normal within two weeks. When she'd told her sorority sisters that her father had promised them all a cruise and charged it to his business account, it had taken almost a month before he'd come around. In the scheme of things, this latest incident should be forgiven, if not forgotten, in three weeks max.

Perhaps she should call him tonight. That way she'd be able to assess his mood and plot her strategy accordingly. After all these years she could tell a lot by the tone of his voice.

"Do you want the room?"

She looked up to find both Tony and Mr. Peeks staring at her.

"Okay." Resigned to the inevitable, Claire reached into her designer bag and pulled out the matching wallet. "I'll take it."

"That'll be forty-five fifty, including tax."

Claire handed him the platinum Visa. At least Daddy had let her keep his credit card. Right before she'd left she'd been worried he was going to ask for it back. He'd started talking about her free ride coming to an end and how it was past time she earned her own way. But thankfully he'd been distracted by a phone call.

"I won't be long." Floyd gestured to the back room. "Mother's got all the credit card stuff with her."

Claire turned to Tony the minute the man left. "His mother? She must be ancient."

Tony chuckled. "I think he's referring to his wife."

"Oh, puh-leeze." Claire rolled her eyes.

"No, I'm serious."

"You don't expect me to really believe he calls his wife 'mother.'"

"Some men do."

"I can tell you one thing," Claire said. "My husband will never call *me* mother."

"I'm 'fraid we got a problem." The door creaked open. Floyd returned with a somber expression on his face. "Visa doesn't like your card."

"What do you mean, doesn't like it?" Claire narrowed her gaze.

"The machine wouldn't take it," Floyd said. "So I called 'em."

He opened a drawer and took out a pair of orange-handled scissors.

"And?" Claire held her breath.

"They told me the account has been closed." He lifted the scissors. "And I was to cut up the card."

"No—"

Before the word fully left her mouth the act was done. Two pieces of silver plastic fell to the counter.

"Why did you do that?" Claire shrieked. "It

was obviously a mistake. Now you've ruined my card.''

"No mistake.'' Floyd shook his head. "They told me to cut it up, and I did.''

Claire ran a shaky hand through her hair, her mind racing. Surely her father wouldn't have closed the account without telling her. A vision of his enraged face the night before she left Cedar Ridge flashed before her. Her shoulders sagged.

"If you have another card I could run that one through," Floyd said.

If only it could be that simple. Unfortunately her billfold was empty. No money. No plastic.

Claire slanted a sideways glance at Tony and raised a brow.

He shook his head slightly and shifted his gaze to the man. "Mr. Peeks, could you give us a few minutes?"

A look of understanding flashed across the motel owner's face. "Ah, sure. Just give a yell when you're ready."

Claire waited until the man had left the room before she spoke.

"Do you have any money you could lend me?" Her cheeks burned hot with humiliation. "I'll pay you back."

"I'd do it in a heartbeat." Tony shifted uncomfortably from one foot to the other. "But I used most of my savings to pay off my school bills and the rest to move here. I get paid at the end of the month, but—"

"You don't have to explain." Claire held up one hand. "You're broke. I'm broke. I get the picture."

She moved to the motel window and looked out on the row of units, unable to believe that she, who just last week had dropped a hundred dollars over lunch without batting an eye, couldn't afford to stay in this fleabag of a motel.

"Life is certainly not fair," she said with a sigh.

"No, it's not."

Claire lifted her gaze. Was that a hint of amusement in his eyes? "You think this is funny?"

"No, of course not." His lips twitched, and his cough sounded suspiciously like a chuckle.

"Yes, you do." Her voice rose in spite of her attempts to control it. "I'm nearly at the end of my rope and you're ready to burst out laughing."

"Oh, Claire." His hand moved to her shoulder.

She jerked away.

"I'm not laughing at you," he said. "But it is funny. Think about it. You're standing there with a two-hundred-dollar Coach purse in your hand, and I have a thirty-thousand-dollar Jeep Cherokee in the parking lot. Yet together we can't scrounge up enough money for a one-night stay."

"At the Shabby Inn." In spite of herself, laughter bubbled up from deep inside Claire. "Forty-five fifty."

"Including tax." Tony's laughter joined hers.

They laughed until tears spilled from their lids and the tension gripping Claire eased.

"But what am I going to do?" She took a deep breath and composed herself, wiping away the last traces of tears from her cheeks.

"God will provide," Tony said softly. "In the meantime, how about some ice cream? I think I have enough for that."

"Ice cream?" Claire glanced at her watch. "It's nearly time for dinner."

"Afraid I'm going to spoil my supper with ice cream, Mother?" Tony said teasingly.

"Don't call me that."

"Mother." The dimple in his cheek flashed.

Claire stepped forward until she stood so close they were almost touching. The smell of his spicy cologne filled her nostrils, and a shiver traveled up her spine. "You're going to pay for that."

He looked down, his brown eyes as dark as the richest chocolate. "What do you have in mind?"

She lifted her face, her gaze focused squarely on his lips. Her breath came in short, shallow puffs.

His head lowered.

"Have you two decided—?"

Tony jerked back. Disappointment surged through Claire, and she turned toward the intruder accusingly.

Red rose up Floyd's neck. He ran a finger inside

his shirt collar as if it had suddenly grown too tight.

"Go ahead. I mean—" Floyd stammered and stopped. The red darkened to crimson.

Beside her Tony smiled, his arm sliding around her waist. "Actually, Mr. Peeks, Claire and I are going to grab something to eat. Then she'll decide what she wants to do."

Claire glanced admiringly at Tony. If her heart wasn't still beating double time she might have believed that they were just talking. "We'll stop back if I decide to take the room."

"Okeydoke," the man said. "Nice to meet you. Reverend, ma'am."

"Nice to meet you, too, Floyd. Maybe I'll see you in church?"

Floyd shrugged. "I guess anything is possible."

Tony laughed and raised a hand in a farewell wave. He ushered Claire through the door, and they headed toward the Jeep.

"Have we even decided where we're going?"

He only smiled.

"You're serious?" She widened her eyes. "We're going to get ice cream?"

That adorable dimple flashed again, and a mischievous look filled his eyes. "Now, Mo—"

Before he could finish, Claire turned, wrapped her arms around him and pressed her mouth to his.

His lips burned against hers. She reveled in the fiery sensation and melted against him.

Finally, they parted. Claire ran a shaky hand through her disheveled hair. She'd kissed more than a few guys in her lifetime, but none had ever made her feel like this.

"Wow," Tony said. "What was that for?"

"Just a little reminder."

"Reminder?"

"That I'm not you're mother." She kept her husky voice to a whisper. "Never have been. Never will be. Is that clear?"

Tony stared thoughtfully for a long moment, a strange glint in his eyes. "Have I ever told you about my learning disability?"

"What are you talking about?" Claire frowned. "What learning disability?"

"My memory sometimes fails me." Now it was his turn to pull her close. "So if I ever call you Mother, feel free to remind me again." His lips brushed hers. "And again."

"You know," she said. "I just might have to do that."

"So what are you going to do?" Tony took a bite of the hot fudge sundae and glanced at Claire.

She took a dainty nibble of her small vanilla cone and wiped her lips with a napkin before answering. "I'm going to call my father when we get back to Mrs. Sandy's and see if he's calmed down."

Tony didn't know the whole story behind Claire leaving Cedar Ridge, but it didn't seem like something that could be mended with a simple phone call. Still, she knew her father better than he did.

"Then what?"

"Then I'll get ready for the party." She took a sip of her soda.

"So you're still planning to go?"

"Wouldn't miss it for the world." Claire smiled. "Don't look so shocked. I told you I'd go and I will."

"I appreciate it."

She waved a dismissive hand. "Actually my social calendar is so wide-open that even a meeting with a bunch of boring church officials sounds appealing."

"What you have on will be fine." Tony knew she'd been worried about what to wear.

"I think not." Claire tossed the rest of her cone into the metal garbage can at the edge of the picnic table and stifled a yawn. "But I'm sure I can find something in my suitcase that will work."

Tony noticed for the first time the lines of fatigue around her eyes. "You never did get your nap."

"That's okay." Claire lifted a large paper cup.

"There's enough caffeine in this cola to keep me going all night."

"Remember Nick and Taylor's engagement party and how we danced until dawn?"

"What I remember is how glad Taylor was to see you." Her lips curved in a smile. "And how jealous Nick was."

Tony shifted uncomfortably. He deeply regretted his involvement in that whole situation. At the time he'd thought Taylor was marrying the wrong man. It wasn't until later he'd realized Claire had only been using him to get to Nick.

She was using you then and she's using you now. Once she's got what she wants, she'll be gone.

He shoved his doubts aside. "How long are you going to stay in Millville?"

"Depends." She flicked a strand of hair over her shoulder. "On how long it takes Daddy to get over being mad. And on how long it takes me to convince him I have a relationship with you."

No longer hungry, Tony tossed the rest of his sundae into the garbage can. It seemed he'd been right to be concerned.

"So once your father believes your lies, you'll be gone." He couldn't quite keep the irritation from his voice.

"Don't go getting all holier-than-thou on me." Claire's dark eyes flashed. "You're no innocent."

Tony started to say that his situation was different, but he stopped himself just in time. A lie was a lie regardless of intent. "You're right. I'll tell them tonight."

"Are you crazy?" Claire's voice was loud and incredulous.

A couple at a nearby table turned to look, and Tony smiled through gritted teeth. "Keep your voice down, please."

"I never said you should come clean." Her eyes were wide with disbelief. "They'll fire you."

"Maybe I deserve it." A knot formed in his stomach. All he'd wanted was to serve God. How had everything gone so wrong?

"Tony." Claire's hand closed over his, and genuine concern filled her eyes. "You didn't lie to them when you interviewed."

"I know," he said with a sigh. "They somehow got the other guy and I mixed up."

"Look, have you ever thought that maybe God wanted you here? That it was His will that you were called to this community? That it was His will that I stopped by when I did?"

"Are you saying that God orchestrated all of this?"

"I don't know," Claire said with a little shrug. "You're the minister. You tell me."

"I can't imagine…"

"Don't they say that God works in mysterious ways?"

Tony reluctantly nodded.

"Think about it. You and I engaged?" She laughed. "It doesn't get much crazier than that."

Chapter Five

Chapter Five

"Could you do me a favor?" Tony cleared his throat and slanted a sideways glance at Claire.

"I'm already doing you one," she said. "Pretending to be your fiancée puts you in my debt, big-time."

He smiled, but a worried look lingered on his face.

The sounds of voices and laughter traveled up the stairs to the landing, and Tony stiffened.

"Okay, spit it out." Claire shot Tony an assessing look. "What's the favor?"

He shifted uncomfortably. "I don't want you to take this the wrong way...."

Claire rolled her eyes. "Just say it."

"You're a beautiful woman." Tony paused for a second before he continued. "You respond to men, they respond to you. I'm not saying there's anything wrong with that.''

"Your point?'' She lifted a brow.

"I don't want you to flirt tonight." His words came out in a rush. "I know it's innocent and all, but I wouldn't want the church council to get the wrong idea."

"Is that the favor?" Her gaze lingered on his broad chest. With his navy chinos and madras shirt with its button-down collar, Tony looked more like a *GQ* model than a small-town minister. He was much too handsome for his own good.

"That's it." He spread his hands. "That's all I ask."

She stared at him for a moment. Why was it so hard to resist a good-looking guy? Claire brushed her lips against his cheek, and the tightness in his jaw eased beneath her touch. "Anything for you, sweetheart."

Claire took a sip of ginger ale and wrinkled her nose. She watched Mrs. Sandy make her way across the crowded living room. Perhaps this was her chance to ask for a nice glass of Merlot.

Before she could even raise the question the landlady buzzed by her without stopping, a harried expression on her face.

Claire considered calling to her, but she thought better of it. The woman was busy. And as long as

Claire was in her gracious mode, she might as well extend that consideration to Mrs. Sandy.

After all, the woman *had* let her use the shower in the maid's quarters and *had* agreed to let her use the room for the night. If she could get her father to wire her some money, perhaps Mrs. Sandy would reconsider her decision to keep the room available for live-in help.

"How do you like Millville?" A woman with mousy brown hair and a pleasant expression smiled and took a seat in the chair opposite Claire.

"You're Dottie? Right?"

The woman flushed with pleasure. "I'm surprised you remembered."

"Your husband owns the hardware store," Claire recited. "And you just had your first baby six months ago."

"I wish I had your memory," Dottie said with an admiring gaze. "I've lived here for almost a year, and I still have trouble with names."

"Where did you live before?" Claire didn't really care, but Dottie was the first woman to go out of her way to talk to her. And since she'd promised Tony she'd steer clear of the men, that left her with few options.

"John grew up in Millville."

The face of a tall, broad-shouldered man somewhere in his late twenties flashed in Claire's mind.

"We met in college and stayed in Denver after

we got married. We'd been there almost eight years before we decided to move back here.''

Claire paused. ''Where did you go to school?''

''The University of Denver.''

''No way.'' Claire's eyes widened in disbelief. ''I graduated from there.''

Although Dottie was several years older than Claire and they had obviously run in different social circles, it was still fun to meet a fellow alumni. To talk to someone who'd been there. Someone who knew the little bistro a few blocks from campus that had been Claire's favorite place to have lunch, and the story behind that certain English professor who had given all the freshman fits.

Dottie might be the before picture in a makeover, but she was sweet and unpretentious, and Claire—who normally wouldn't have given the woman a second glance—found herself enjoying their conversation.

''You doing okay?'' Tony stopped next to Claire's chair, and his hand dropped to rest lightly on her shoulder.

A shiver traveled up her spine. Claire lifted her face and smiled. ''Fine. How about you?''

''Great.'' He nodded. ''I'm enjoying getting to know everybody.''

''Dottie and I were just talking about the University of Denver.'' At his blank look, she added, ''Where I went to school.''

"Right." The dimple in his cheek flashed before his gaze shifted to a tall man across the room waving him over. "I'll be back in a few minutes."

"Take your time," Claire said, and found she meant the words. It had been a stressful day, and Dottie was like a soothing tonic to her frazzled nerves.

"He sure is handsome." Dottie's gaze followed Tony across the room before returning to Claire. "But then you're a beautiful woman. You two make such a perfect couple."

Claire's lips curved in a satisfied smile. Dottie was right. She and Tony *were* the best-looking couple in the room. The only other pair that even came close was Adam and Jocelyn.

Claire caught sight of the willowy blonde making her way across the room. Her lips tightened. She'd already been introduced to Jocelyn Wingate, and Claire hadn't been overly impressed. The woman was attractive and stylish but seemed too taken with her own self-importance.

Right after they were introduced, she'd had to mention that not only was her husband on the church council, he was also the mayor of Millville. *Mayor of Millville.* Claire choked back a snort of laughter.

Another big fish in a small pond.

"Claire!" Jocelyn collapsed into a nearby chair and greeted Claire like they were old friends. "I've talked my little brains out, and I'm simply exhausted.''

Claire raised a brow and bit back a pithy retort. Why had she ever promised Tony she'd be good tonight?

''I saw you over here all by your lonesome and thought I'd come over.''

Out of the corner of her eye, Claire saw Dottie's face redden. It was true that the attractive Jocelyn would normally be more Claire's type than the plain Jane she'd been visiting with, but still Dottie had been nothing but kind. Claire refused to let the comment go by unchallenged and relished the idea of taking Jocelyn down a peg in the process.

''Actually I wasn't alone, Jocelyn. Dottie and I have been talking.''

Jocelyn's gaze shifted to Dottie, and a smile that didn't quite reach her eyes lifted the blonde's lips. ''Why, I didn't see you over there.''

Jocelyn's wide-eyed innocence didn't fool Claire in the least. She'd used that same trick too often not to recognize it.

Dottie smiled pleasantly and took a sip of her tea. ''Really? I've been here the whole time.''

Claire's estimation of Dottie inched up a notch. She liked people with spunk.

''You're fortunate to be able to mix right in with your surroundings.'' Jocelyn laughed. ''I couldn't blend into the woodwork if I tried.''

A surge of unexpected anger swept through Claire, tempered by the truth of Jocelyn's words. She glanced at Dottie and shot her a reassuring smile.

Dottie *was* nondescript and could easily be overlooked. Jocelyn, with her long blond hair, big blue eyes and angelic face, would be noticed in any crowd.

It wasn't the accuracy of the words that bothered Claire, it was the way they were delivered. Although not necessarily malicious, they were spoken with no thought or concern given to the other person's feelings.

The callous disregard hit home and reminded Claire of another woman who often spoke before she thought. She shifted uncomfortably in her seat and shook aside the momentary discomfort. She may have been blunt at times, occasionally outspoken, but had she ever been deliberately cruel? Not that she could recall, anyway. But a voice in the back of her head noted her memory was nothing if not convenient.

It didn't matter at the moment. After all, it was Jocelyn's behavior under scrutiny right now.

"How do you like Millville so far?" Jocelyn asked, seemingly oblivious to the tension in the air.

"Actually, I haven't seen that much of it," Claire said tersely. "I just got here today."

"Let me give you some advice." Jocelyn leaned

forward. She whispered conspiratorially but loud enough to easily be heard. "Don't expect too much and you won't be disappointed."

In spite of herself, Claire's lips twitched.

"How can you say that?" Dottie said indignantly, obviously forgetting that Jocelyn had directed the comment to Claire and not to her. "Millville is a wonderful town."

"Spoken like a true Chamber of Commerce member." To Claire's surprise, instead of being upset at Dottie's intrusion or the censure in her tone, Jocelyn laughed. "You sound just like Adam. He says to give it time. Says I'm going to love the town. Well, I've been here six years and I still can't say that I love it."

Dottie opened her mouth, but Claire spoke first, putting an end to any further discussion of the town and its virtues. How much could you say about a town with a population under a thousand?

"I take it you're not from here?" Claire asked.

"I'm from Chicago." Jocelyn smiled, her teeth perfectly straight and white. "Adam and I met at Northwestern."

"A good friend of mine, Kelly St. John, went there," Claire said. "I know it's a big school, so I don't suppose you—"

"Oh, my goodness." Jocelyn clasped a hand to her chest. "Kelly and I used to hang out together all the time."

Jocelyn chattered nonstop, and Claire discovered not only did they know many of the same people, but Adam had once interned at a company in Chicago owned by Claire's father.

"It's such a small world," Jocelyn said. "I can't believe how much we have in common."

It was true. Still, as shocking as it was, she liked Dottie more than she liked Jocelyn. And more than she liked herself.

Dottie shifted in her seat, the bright smile still on her face but fading fast.

Claire widened her smile to encompass both Dottie and Jocelyn. "It is amazing how we've all connected."

"We'll have to go out sometime soon," Jocelyn announced. "Drive to Des Moines for dinner and a movie or maybe go on a picnic."

"Either beats sitting around doing nothing. Count me in," Claire said. "What about you, Dottie?"

Dottie hesitated, and Claire glanced pointedly at Jocelyn.

"C'mon, Dottie," Jocelyn said. "It'll be fun."

"I have to ask John." Dottie smiled tentatively. "But I'm sure it will be okay. As long as I can get a baby-sitter."

"What are you ladies cooking up?" Adam Wingate's smile included all three women.

The mayor was an attractive man around thirty

with light brown hair and twinkling green eyes. For someone so young he already had the polished manner of a politician down pat.

"I've told Claire and Dottie we have to get together. If you guys are nice we might even let you come along. Let you take us out to dinner," Jocelyn said. "Or maybe if the weather holds we could do a picnic."

Even considering the ants and bugs, a picnic sounded better to Claire than a trip to Des Moines. What kind of name was that for a town, anyway? And why even have the S at the end of each word if you weren't going to pronounce it?

"If we had a picnic we could make fried chicken," Dottie said eagerly. "And potato salad."

Claire could only stare. Surely the woman didn't plan to make it herself? After all, that's what KFC was for.

"We have the cabin on Hampton Lake." Jocelyn's gaze shifted to Adam. "We could take the ski boat out."

"Whatever you all decide is fine with me," Adam said. "John and I were friends in high school. It'd be great to get together. Plus this would be a good opportunity for us to get to know our new pastor better. And, of course—" Adam smiled at Claire "—his bride-to-be."

"Whose bride?" Tony's rich baritone sounded behind Claire.

"Your beautiful fiancée is filling your social calendar," Adam said with an easy laugh.

Tony's gaze settled on Claire, and she could read the approval in his eyes. "Whatever Claire decides is okay. My schedule's wide-open."

"Pastor, could you come over here a minute?" Mrs. Sandy called to Tony from across the room. "You, too, Mr. Mayor."

The two men had barely left when Dottie rose. "If you'll excuse me, I need to call the sitter."

She disappeared into the kitchen, leaving Jocelyn and Claire alone.

"Adam seems like a nice guy," Claire said.

"He is." An unmistakable look of love filled Jocelyn's eyes. "He's got more friends than anyone I know. His family has been here for five generations. He's one of them. I, on the other hand..."

"Don't tell me." Claire held up a hand. "You're the outsider?"

"You got it. And believe me, this is a new experience for me. Usually I don't have any trouble fitting in." Jocelyn shrugged, but Claire could see the hurt reflected in her blue eyes. "But here—" she paused "—sometimes I wonder if I'll ever fit in."

"I say if they don't like you, who needs them?" Claire took a sip of her drink. "It's their loss."

"Exactly." Jocelyn lifted her glass and clinked it against Claire's. "I'm glad you're moving here, Claire. I think you and I could be good friends."

Surprisingly, despite her rather negative first impression, Claire had to agree. It was too bad she wouldn't be around long enough for that friendship to bloom.

"Tell me what you know about the people here tonight." Claire's gaze swept the crowd. She'd learned long ago from her father the importance of scouting the opposition. If Tony was to retain his position, he needed to know the score. "And don't leave out anything."

"What'd he say?" Tony pulled a chair next to Claire and sat down.

"Not a whole lot." Claire glanced around and changed the subject. "Where's the landlady?"

"In bed. She was dead on her feet. Said to tell you good-night."

It was almost midnight, and the members of the church council and their spouses had long since left. Claire had been on the phone with her father when Tony had started helping Mrs. Sandy with the cleanup.

They'd just got the dishes cleared when Claire had motioned Mrs. Sandy into the den. Tony had been curious to find out how Claire's father had responded to her call, but Claire had made it clear when she'd slammed the door in his face that she wanted to talk to Mrs. Sandy alone. So he'd finished loading the dishwasher instead.

"I'm surprised she went to bed before dawn. The woman is a workaholic."

"I think she has to be to make ends meet." Tony glanced curiously at Claire. He didn't want to talk about Darlene Sandy. He wanted to talk about Claire. And her father. And that all too brief phone call she'd made from the den. It had barely lasted five minutes. He didn't know if that was a good sign or not. "How was your father?"

Claire shrugged and studied her long red nails. Tony reached over and took one of her hands. "What did he say?"

"I don't want to talk about it." She pulled her hand from his and brushed her hair from her face. "I'd kill for a couple of Dove bars right now."

"Dove bars?" Tony frowned.

"Sometimes a woman just needs chocolate." She drew a ragged breath. "This is one of those times."

"You want me to see if Mrs. Sandy has any in her freezer?"

Claire shook her head. "I already looked. All she has are ice-milk bars." A look of disgust crossed her face. "Why even bother?"

"What did your father say?" The ice cream

wasn't important. She was just trying to change the subject, but he wouldn't let her.

"Nothing that I didn't already know." She stood and turned her face to the darkened window so all he could see was her reflection in the glass. "He told me what a big disappointment I was. Asked me how a man could succeed in every other part of his life, but be such a failure in raising a daughter."

"How did that make you feel?" He'd never particularly liked the phrase. But it had been drilled into him during his counseling classes at the seminary, and it popped out automatically.

Claire whirled. "How do you think that made me feel?"

Hurt mixed with anger on her face, and he knew he'd better tread cautiously. "I think it must have been hard."

She plopped down in the chair and blew out a harsh breath. "I thought I meant something to him. I thought he cared about me."

"I'm sure he loves you," Tony said gently. "Maybe you caught him at a bad time."

"I should have known you'd take his side. You men are all alike." Claire snorted in disgust. "Wouldn't you think he'd have been glad to hear from me? To know I was okay? Instead he immediately starts babbling about this important conference call he has scheduled and how he needs to keep the line free.''

''Did you get a chance to ask him about the money?'' Ever since the credit card incident Tony knew the money worry had been foremost in Claire's mind.

''I asked him.'' Claire's lips tightened.

''And?''

''He said no.'' She met his gaze. ''He didn't ask any questions, didn't want to know why I needed it, just kept talking about that stupid conference call.''

There was a lot he could have said, but he sensed this wasn't the time for platitudes. He patted the spot next to him on the sofa. ''Sit by me.''

She shook her head and crossed her arms across her chest.

''C'mon.'' He shot her his most engaging grin. ''I promise I won't bite.''

Indecision showed on her face before she took a few steps and sat beside him. The light floral scent of her perfume wafted about him.

He inhaled. ''You smell great.''

''According to Daddy that's all I'm good for,'' she said with more than a hint of bitterness in her tone. ''Looking good, smelling good, being a trophy on some guy's arm.''

Tony knew Henry Waters. Although he could see Henry thinking such thoughts, he couldn't imagine him ever saying them. Especially not to his own daughter. "I can't believe your father said that."

She shrugged. "Maybe he didn't say those exact words, but that's what he meant."

"It doesn't make sense." Tony shook his head. "He knows what you're capable of. Why, you practically ran his advertising department."

"Doesn't count," she said with more than a hint of dramatics. "I was working for him. That's not the real world."

"What about your time in D.C.?" He and Claire had met at a party when she'd first moved to Washington. She'd worked for a public relations firm, and he'd been at loose ends then, not sure what he wanted to do with his life.

"I'm sure he's written it off as some sort of fluke." Claire heaved a heavy sigh. "The man has his mind made up, and there's no changing it."

"Did you tell him about us?" Surely the man would be happy his daughter had fallen in love.... Tony stopped and reminded himself that love wasn't part of this picture.

"He didn't care." Claire waved a dismissive hand. "He gave it three weeks. Said either I'd be sick of you by then or you'd be sick of me. Said he'd seen it happen too often in the past to think this time would be any different."

Tony grabbed her hand and brought it to his lips. "Well, we're just going to have to show him."

Claire's expression was clearly skeptical. "You think we could actually make it four weeks without killing each other?"

"Four weeks? Piece of cake." Excitement surged through Tony. If she stayed in Millville for a month, that should be more than enough time to convince the church council what an asset he could be to the community and to the congregation.

"I don't know. It would be a record for me." Claire laughed, and her dark eyes sparkled. Tony couldn't help but think how pretty she looked.

"I know you'd rather be anywhere but here," he said in a soft voice. "But I am glad you're staying."

"Of course you are," Claire said. "The longer I'm here, the better it is for you."

Tony had to admit that was part of it, but nowhere near the whole story. He liked having Claire around. She was like a breath of fresh air. Funny he'd never thought of her in that way before. "By the way, you did a great job tonight."

"I almost went into withdrawal," she said with a twinkle in her eye. "No deep voices, no sports stories, no pats on the butt. I'm not used to hanging around women."

"Adam said you're the first woman Jocelyn has

warmed up to since she moved to Millville. And John told me Dottie thought you were wonderful.''

"Be careful. All those compliments will go to my head.'' Claire rubbed her forehead with one hand.

Tony narrowed his gaze. "Do you have a headache?''

"That father of mine would give anyone a headache.'' Claire winced.

"Miss Waters, this is your lucky day,'' Tony said. "I know just what you need.'' He reached over and turned down the light. "Slide a little closer.''

"Is this part of your ministerial duties?''

"Not exactly, but you can trust me.'' Tony gently turned her shoulders, and his hands moved to her neck. His fingers slid inside the collar of her silk shirt, massaging her tense muscles.

"So this is what you meant.''

"What else?'' He chuckled.

Several minutes passed before he felt her finally relax. With her eyes shut and a pleased smile on her lips, Claire looked like a cat that just drank a saucer of cream and was ready to lie in the sun.

"See,'' he said softly under his breath, "there are some benefits to being in Millville.''

"And to being your fiancée?'' She opened her eyes and tilted her head back.

His lips brushed her ear. "That, too.''

"You're not playing fair." Claire turned to face him, and in the dim light her eyes smoldered like burning coals.

"I'm not playing at all." He gently brushed her mouth with his lips. "I like you."

She wrapped her arms around his neck.

Tony pulled her close and did what he'd wanted to do all evening. He kissed her slowly, lingeringly. "You're a wonderful woman, Claire. Don't let your father or anyone tell you differently."

Claire smiled. "And you're a nice guy, Tony. This town would be crazy not to want you."

"Crazy, huh?" Tony returned her smile. He had to admit he liked having her in his corner. In a way, he could see why the church council preferred married ministers. A supportive spouse by your side could be a substantial advantage.

He shoved the thought aside and reminded himself he could do God's will, single or married.

"Actually," he added, "what's crazy is us acting like a couple of high school kids, kissing on the couch."

"I doubt anyone would find fault with these simple kisses." Claire peered at him from beneath lowered lashes. "They're about as exciting as kissing your brother."

"Kissing me is like kissing a brother?" His voice rose.

"Uh-huh," Claire said, her eyes wide and innocent.

He turned her face to his and slipped his other arm around her, pulling her tight against him. This time when his mouth lowered to hers, he wasn't content to brush her lips lightly, softly. The minute their lips met, he lost himself in the warm sweetness. His hand moved up, his fingers raking through her hair, pulling her closer still.

His heart raced. The creak on the stairs barely registered.

"Well, well, what do we have here?"

Tony jerked back. His gaze darted to the doorway.

"The minister and the maid." April stood in the doorway, a smug smile on her face. Her gaze shifted between Tony and Claire. "Sort of sounds like a bad romance novel."

"It does have a certain ring to it," he said lightly. "Although I'm not sure where the maid part comes in."

"Didn't Mom tell you?" April's gaze shifted to Claire. "Claire is our new maid."

Chapter Six

The pounding on the door matched the pounding in Claire's temples. The headache she always got when she didn't get enough sleep hit her full force. She pushed herself up on her elbows and craned her neck to see the clock. Six-thirty.

She groaned and plopped back onto the soft mattress, pulling the covers over her head.

"Claire, it's Mrs. Sandy." Despite the thickness of the hardwood, the woman's voice carried easily through the door. "Are you awake?"

"I am now," she muttered.

"Claire?"

"Just a minute." She shoved aside the covers and swung her bare legs over the side of the bed. Her skin turned to gooseflesh in the cool morning air, and she clenched her jaw. What in the world could be so important that you'd have to wake someone in the middle of the night?

"Claire?" The rapping sounded again.

Claire's head pounded a response.

"Coming." She stumbled toward the door, not even bothering to grab a robe.

Claire fumbled with the lock, impatiently shoving aside a strand of hair that dared to fall forward and block her view. Just when she was ready to scream in frustration, the bolt sprang open with a click.

She jerked the door open, the sudden movement setting off a fresh wave of pain in her head.

"Good morning." Mrs. Sandy beamed.

Claire's stomach clenched. How could anyone abide such cheerfulness at such an early hour? "Is something the matter?"

"Matter?" Confusion clouded the woman's face.

"You're up so early."

"Early?" Mrs. Sandy laughed. "I've been up for over an hour. I just took my first batch of cinnamon rolls out of the oven."

For the first time Claire noted the tantalizing aroma that hung in the air. "Thanks, but I'll eat later."

The woman mouthed a protest, but Claire paid no attention. She needed sleep more than food. Her gaze shifted to the bed. If she was lucky, she could easily get in another four or five hours.

Claire started to push the door closed, but Mrs. Sandy's foot stopped it.

"I don't think you understand." Mrs. Sandy smiled, but her gaze was firm. "I need you to help me serve this morning. The guests will start coming down around seven."

Serving? As in servant? Claire cringed. It was true she'd agreed to help out in exchange for the room. She hadn't had a choice. But she'd hoped the landlady would at least give her a few days' reprieve.

As if she could read Claire's mind, Mrs. Sandy's gaze softened. "I know you were up late. And I hate to ask, but April's not feeling well this morning, and I really do need the help."

Plus, you did agree. The words hung unspoken in the air, and Claire knew she had no choice.

"I need to shower." If she was lucky that could buy her a couple of hours.

"That's no problem." Mrs. Sandy glanced at her watch. "Ten till seven should be good enough. I'll see you then."

Without another word, Mrs. Sandy turned on her heel and headed down the hall.

Twenty minutes? Claire watched the retreating form in disbelief. The woman actually expected her to get ready in *twenty minutes?*

Claire managed to trim her hour-and-a-half morning ritual to twenty-two minutes. Her hair hung in loose tendrils down her back, still slightly damp from her brief shower. Her makeup had been reduced to the bare minimum—a little foundation, a dusting of blush and a few swipes of mascara.

Surprisingly, when she caught a glimpse of her reflection in the mirror on her way out the door, she liked what she saw. She looked younger than her twenty-eight years and…wholesome. A word she'd never thought of before in connection with herself, but one that in this instance fit perfectly.

Thanks to the three Advil she'd swallowed the minute Mrs. Sandy had left, the pain in her head had lessened to a faint twinge.

Claire pulled the door shut and glanced at her tangerine-colored checked shirt and khaki pants. She wasn't sure what to wear. All she knew was she'd sleep on the streets before she'd ever let those ridiculous black and white outfits her father's household help wore touch her skin.

See what you've done to me, Daddy? I hope you're satisfied.

Claire swallowed hard and refused to give in to the wave of despair that washed over her. On top of everything, today was her birthday, and no one even knew it. She doubted if anyone would even care. After all, her own father hadn't even mentioned it yesterday on the phone. In the past he'd always planned elaborate celebrations. But that was then and this was now. And she was looking at not only no party, but a day filled with physical work.

She shifted her eyes heavenward. Perhaps she'd been asking the wrong father for help. Since her earthly father had turned out to be such a disappointment, it might be time to turn to someone else.

Dear Father, You know how much I hate manual labor. Please help me.

Claire knew the prayer was self-serving. Most of her requests were. But if you weren't going to be honest when you prayed, what was the point?

Besides, He would know.

Tony rolled over and hit the alarm. He lay still for a moment trying to recapture the dream. A smile lingered on his lips. Claire. Her skin had been silky to his touch, her lips warm and inviting.

Outside his window a bird chirped its own wakeup call. He shifted his gaze and took note of the clear blue sky. All signs pointed to another beautiful day. The weather was more suited to June than mid-May.

Mid-May. Tony frowned. He jumped out of bed and headed across the floor in his bare feet. Flipping open his planner, he breathed a sign of relief. Thank goodness he'd remembered. Tomorrow would have been too late. He reached for the phone and punched in the number.

"Hello." The familiar voice brought a smile to his face. He made a mental note to call the florist and order flowers.

"Mother, it's Tony." He dropped into the chair and put his feet on the desk. "Happy birthday."

"Why, sweetheart." Pleasure ran through his mother's voice and made him glad he'd taken the time to call. "I didn't expect to hear from you."

"Why not? It's May fourteenth," he said. Despite her words, he knew she would have been disappointed if he hadn't called. "Who else do I know that has a birthday today?"

Claire. Her image popped unbidden into his mind.

"I'm so glad you called. I know you must be busy," she said. "How's Iowa?"

They talked for a few more minutes, trying to arrange a time when his parents could come to Millville.

"The parsonage should be completely renovated by July," Tony said. "Assuming everything goes as scheduled. But you're welcome to come anytime." Of course where they would stay if they came before the parsonage was complete was another matter. But knowing his father's tight business schedule, he'd take them whenever he could get them.

"We're anxious to see where you'll be living." His mother paused. "We're going to be visiting Grandmama the last week in June. How about if we plan to spend the Fourth of July holiday with you?"

"That'd be great." He'd definitely be settled in by then. Assuming the church officials hadn't fired him first. "Why don't you bring Grandmama with you?"

Grandmama was his mother's grandmother and one of Tony's favorite people. She lived in a little town by the Illinois-Iowa border. On his way to Millville, Tony had stopped and spent a few days with her.

"I don't know, Tony. She's ninety-six and doesn't travel much anymore. I'm not sure how she'd handle the trip."

"It's not that far," Tony said. "Besides, when I saw her she didn't look a day over seventy-five."

"I know now why she adores you." His mother laughed. "She must have told me a dozen times how much she enjoyed your visit."

"We had a good time." He remembered how his great-grandmother's eyes had sparkled when he'd taken her for ice cream and a drive around the town square.

"She told me she'd given you her ring."

The ornate piece had been a love offering from his great-grandfather to his new bride. Crafted in the early part of the twentieth century, the large stone was brilliant and would have been perfect except for several tiny dark specks marring its clarity.

Grandmama called the specks trouble spots. Said all couples face problems in their married life and that for over seventy years the ring had served as a reminder to her to focus on the big picture and not dwell on the little problems.

"She insisted I take it," Tony said. "I'll give it to you when you come."

"No, you won't," his mother said firmly. "She wants you to have it. One of these days you'll find that special woman, and then you'll need an engagement ring."

Everyone thinks I've already found her.

Tony suddenly realized that although Claire was supposed to be his fiancée, he'd never given her a ring.

"I think that time is still down the road," Tony said with a laugh. "And anyway the odds are, when I do find her, she'll probably want a different ring."

"When you find the right woman—" his mother paused as if choosing her words carefully "—I hope she'll be the kind of woman who will appreciate and love Grandmama's ring."

"Maybe," Tony said doubtfully. "I guess we'll just have to wait and see."

* * *

"Miss, could I have a little more coffee?" A man at the far end of the table raised his cup.

Claire heaved an exasperated sigh and cast a pointed glance at the coffeepot on the warmer sitting two feet from the guy.

"On second thought—" he pushed back his chair and stood "—I can get it myself."

"Ma'am." A young mother close to Claire's age motioned to her. "Justin spilled his orange juice. Could you get him another glass?"

The three-year-old boy beamed at Claire, not a hint of contrition on his chubby face. "More juice."

At any other time she might have smiled. Or given some thanks that at least the woman had cleaned up the spill herself. But it had been a short night and a long morning, and at this moment Claire didn't feel at all thankful.

She shifted her gaze to the woman and stared.

"We're running late, so if you could hurry, I'd really appreciate it." Unlike the man, this woman didn't back down.

"We'll get that juice for your son right away, Mrs. Andrews." Mrs. Sandy's voice sounded behind her.

She hadn't heard the landlady come in. For a second Claire wondered how long Mrs. Sandy had been standing there. Then she decided she didn't care.

"Claire, will you get that for me, please?"

Claire turned and met Mrs. Sandy's gaze. "Of course."

Her open palm slapped the door leading to the kitchen. Claire left the room without a backward glance.

Mrs. Sandy's words may have been framed as a question, but there'd been no mistaking the message. Claire jerked the large plastic bottle of country style orange juice from the refrigerator.

How could her life have taken such a downward turn in such a short time? She'd considered telling the landlady it was her birthday, but she'd probably only hand her a scrub brush. The only thing she could hope was that it didn't get any worse. She couldn't take much more.

But through the course of the day she learned she could. If Claire wanted to be honest she'd have to admit that Mrs. Sandy hadn't asked her to do anything she wasn't willing to do herself. They'd worked side by side cleaning the upstairs bathrooms. Claire's stomach churned just thinking about it. She'd done her best to skim the surface, but Mrs. Sandy's eagle eyes had missed nothing.

The second time the landlady had made her go back and redo the shower, Claire had almost snapped and told the woman exactly what she could do with her job. Only the thought that she had nowhere else to stay made her bite her tongue.

And still the day continued to get worse. Claire sat in the overstuffed chair and tried to rein in her mounting anger.

Tony was five minutes late, and being kept waiting was the last thing Claire needed after the day she'd endured.

Today should have been special. Instead she'd been treated like Cinderella, with Mrs. Sandy playing the role of evil stepmother to perfection.

She glanced at the clock again. Seven minutes late. Her already tightly strung nerves quivered, her irritation fueled by the knowledge that while she'd been slaving away, Tony had been out enjoying himself.

When he'd sauntered into the kitchen around lunchtime Claire thought he'd been about to ask her to run errands with him. But when Mrs. Sandy mentioned everything she and Claire needed to get done before the barbecue, Tony had merely brushed a kiss across her forehead, murmured something about hoping she had a good day and left.

Good day? She snorted. Yeah, it had been swell.

The door creaked open, and she looked up.

"You're late," she snapped.

"Hello to you, too." Tony flashed her an engaging smile. "How was your day?"

She narrowed her gaze. He looked happy. Excited, even. Her irritation inched up a notch.

"Horrible," she said. "How was yours?"

He shifted uneasily, and his smile dimmed. For a second Claire experienced a twinge of regret. She knew she shouldn't take out her bad mood on Tony, but for some reason she couldn't seem to stop.

"I have something for you," he said. "Hold out your hand."

She kept her hand at her side. "Unless it's a million dollars, I don't want it."

"Claire, hold out your hand." An edge of steel that she'd never heard before ran through his voice.

Who did he think he was to order her around? Claire glared at him, but he didn't flinch.

She extended her hand palm up. He dropped a tiny box into her grasp, the dark velvet soft against her skin. Claire lifted her gaze. Her lips curved upward in a smile. "A gift?"

"I guess you could say that."

His expression was wary, and she wanted to tell him not to worry. She adored expensive jewelry.

Claire flipped open the box and stared, stunned.

"It's my great-grandmother's ring," he said quickly. "You needed an engagement ring so I thought this would do. Unfortunately it's a family heirloom, so you can't keep—"

"Keep it?" Claire glanced at the gem, disappointment squeezing her chest and making it hard for her to breathe. "Why would I want to do that? It's not exactly my style."

Tony's jaw tightened, and the last bit of light faded from his eyes. "If you feel that way..."

"Really, I didn't mean it the way it sounded." Awkwardly she cleared her throat, and a wave of guilt washed over her. She always had a tendency to say what she thought, but this time she knew she'd gone too far.

"It's okay." He reached for the ring, and she knew it wasn't okay. Not by a long shot.

"Pastor, I've got everything arranged. They all..." Mrs. Sandy's gaze shot to Claire, and her voice trailed off. "Hello, Claire. I didn't see you sitting there."

The landlady's gaze shifted to the diamond in Claire's hand. "Oh, my, how beautiful."

Claire managed to force a little smile.

"We'd been wondering why Claire didn't wear an engagement ring." Mrs. Sandy's gaze shifted to Tony. "I guess now we know why you were waiting."

Tony's smile didn't quite reach his eyes, but Claire doubted Mrs. Sandy noticed. The woman wasn't paying attention to anything but the large solitaire.

"It's exquisite." She turned to Claire. "I bet you love it, don't you?"

"I do." Claire wondered if God would strike her dead for lying. But then she reminded herself He never had before.

"Does it fit?"

"I don't know." Claire glanced at Tony. "I haven't had a chance to try it on."

Claire started to take the ring from its case, but Mrs. Sandy's hand stopped her.

"No, my dear," the woman said softly. "Let Tony put it on you."

Tony reached for the ring, his eyes flat and expressionless. She remembered how happy he'd been when he'd first pulled out the case. But what had she done wrong? She'd only been honest.

The diamond slid on her finger.

"It fits perfectly." Claire was unable to keep the surprise from her voice. She wore a five and always had to have her rings sized down. Her gaze shifted to the gem. It looked a little better on her finger than in the box. The antique setting was unique, and the stone was large enough to be acceptable. If not for those scattered dark specks, it would have been more than adequate.

"Looks like it was made to be on your finger," Mrs. Sandy said with a dreamy expression on her face.

Claire glanced at Tony. A chill traveled up her spine at the tightness in his jaw. Maybe she should have tried to soften her words, but who'd have thought he would have taken it this way?

She realized at that moment that she didn't know Tony Karelli half as well as she'd thought she did.

"I'll leave you two alone." Mrs. Sandy patted Claire's hand and bustled from the room. "Don't forget the barbecue starts at seven."

Claire waited until the woman was out of sight before she spoke. "Tony, I didn't mean—"

"Forget it." He waved a dismissive hand and jerked to his feet. "It doesn't matter."

In silence she watched him leave the room, and she couldn't help but feel she'd make a big mistake, that for whatever reason, it really did matter.

"Where's Tony?" Jocelyn's gaze scanned the crowd.

"Mingling over there." Claire loosely pointed across the room and took a sip of her soda. What would Jocelyn say if Claire told her the truth, that she and Tony had barely exchanged five words all evening?

During the first hour or two, she'd just suspected he was avoiding her. Now she was certain. All this because she'd made a simple observation about the ring. It wasn't as if he had bought it for her. Actually, given its flaws, she couldn't imagine anyone paying good money for it.

Surprisingly no one had said anything derogatory about the ring, at least not yet.

"Is that a diamond I see on your finger?" Jocelyn's eyes sparkled as bright as the gem on Claire's finger. "Hold it up. Let me see it."

Claire's heart sank. She reluctantly lifted her hand to the light.

With the manner of a professional gemologist, Jocelyn leaned forward to study the stone, her gaze narrowing. She studied the ring for several seconds in silence.

"It's beautiful, Claire." Jocelyn paused. "And so unique."

The fact that the woman was being ten times more tactful than Claire had been to Tony infuriated Claire. She could recognize the pity in Jocelyn's eyes.

The woman could afford to be kind. That three-carat solitaire gracing Jocelyn's finger was gorgeous. Flawless.

"It's a family heirloom," Claire said at last. "The sentiment is what makes it truly priceless."

She could barely choke the words out, the concept she was espousing was so foreign. She'd never been one for all that hearts-and-flowers drivel.

"Of course," Jocelyn said as if she really did understand. "Of course it does."

Claire chatted with Jocelyn for a few more

minutes, thankful when the woman finally left to find her husband.

"Hello." Dottie tapped Claire on the shoulder. "Having a good time?"

"Dottie." Claire breathed a sigh of relief and smiled her first genuine smile of the evening. "I've been looking for you."

It wasn't far from the truth. Dottie was one of the few people Claire didn't dread seeing. "Did you just get here?"

"Our baby-sitter showed up an hour late." A wry grin twisted Dottie's mouth. "Just wait until you and Tony have children. You'll find that it's the baby-sitter who controls your life."

Claire laughed, and an image of a dark-haired baby flashed in her mind. "It's hard for me to imagine getting married, let alone having children."

"You just wait," Dottie said with a teasing grin. "I thought that, too. But once you're married and settled in those baby thoughts just seem to come naturally."

"I'll take your word for it." Claire brushed away a strand of hair with the back of her hand.

"Is that the ring?" Dottie's eyes widened. "Mrs. Sandy said it was beautiful, but it's more than that, it's gorgeous."

Claire scanned Dottie's face, but all she saw was open admiration. She lifted her hand.

"The setting is so intricate." Dottie's finger traced a filigreed side. "I wondered why you didn't have it yesterday, but then Mrs. Sandy explained why Tony wanted to give it to you today—"

Dottie clapped a hand over her mouth.

"That's okay," Claire said. "Tony *did* want me to have the ring before the party."

"I saw him over by the punch bowl when we first came in, and he told me how it had been his great-grandmother's ring. Told me she'd wanted him to give to the woman he loved."

"He told you that?" That was more than he'd told her. Of course, she hadn't really given him a chance.

"Don't be mad." Dottie ducked her head, and a hint of red crept up her neck. "We were talking about what I call gifts of the heart. I told him how I never even had a diamond when John and I were first married. We didn't have the money. All we could afford was this gold band."

This time it was Dottie who held out her hand. A simple ring encircled her finger.

"It's lovely," Claire said automatically.

"Not really," Dottie smiled. "But it means the world to me. I love it because of the feeling behind it. It's a gift of the heart. You understand."

Claire nodded. She did understand. At least a little, and a lot more than she would have in the past.

"I'd like everyone's attention." Mrs. Sandy clapped her hands, and to Claire's surprise the room quieted immediately. Tony stood to the side with a smile that to Claire looked forced. Mrs. Sandy's gaze scanned the crowd. "Where's Claire?"

Suddenly she found herself being pushed forward through the crowd until she stood next to Tony and Mrs. Sandy.

The woman wrapped an arm around Claire, forcing her to face the crowd. "When I asked our new pastor what he'd like for the barbecue, he had only one request. A cake."

Claire slanted a sideways glance at Tony, but he refused to meet her gaze.

"And not just any cake," Mrs. Sandy continued. "He wanted a birthday cake for his fiancée."

"Happy birthday, Claire." Dottie came out of the kitchen holding aloft a triple-layer chocolate cake ablaze with candles.

All at once a rousing chorus of "Happy Birthday to You" broke out and filled the house.

Claire's throat tightened. She'd reconciled herself that this year her birthday would come and go without any fanfare. After all, her father hadn't even remembered when she'd talked to him yesterday. Tears stung the back of her lids.

"Happy birthday, sweetheart."

To the crowd, Tony's wishes sounded sincere.

Only Claire knew his lips were cold and his eyes lacked the warmth that had been there only a few hours before.

"How did—?"

"Isn't it amazing," Mrs. Sandy chirped. "You and Tony's mother having the same birthday."

Of course. Now she understood how, but why?

Because he's a nice guy, a tiny voice inside Claire whispered. A nice guy that didn't deserve the way he'd been treated. A nice guy *she* didn't deserve.

Mrs. Sandy handed her a plate with a piece of cake. "Tony told me this afternoon to make sure you got the one with the rose."

Her gaze dropped. On top of the cake, formed out of sugar, was one perfect red rose. A flower that matched the filigreed one on her ring.

Her throat tightened. Claire poked at the flower with a fork and her eyes blurred.

Abruptly she realized her father had been right all along. It was time for her to make some changes.

Chapter Seven

Claire rolled over and punched the pillow with her fist. How was it she could be so exhausted but still be unable to sleep?

She breathed slowly in and out and tried for several minutes to will herself to dreamland. When the clock struck two, Claire gave in to the inevitable. She shoved back the covers and slipped out of bed, sliding her feet into a pair of blue fluffy mules at the bedside. Instead of reaching for the kimono that matched her skimpy pajamas, Claire grabbed the thick chenille robe. If she was going outside, she'd need something a little warmer than silk. She'd been plagued by insomnia long enough to know that the only thing that would help her relax was to walk off her tension.

She made her way to the foyer and out the front

door without waking anyone. Crisp and cool, the night air seemed more suited to fall than late spring. Claire pulled the robe tightly around her, cinched it closed with the belt and stepped to the porch railing.

A thousand stars glittered from the night sky, and the moon looked like a perfectly round yellow globe suspended in midair. Despite the chill, Claire felt a tingle of anticipation. Though it made no sense, it seemed somehow right to be standing where she was at this moment, breathing in the fresh air of the heartland, admiring the beauty of the night.

God's in His heaven and all's right with the world.

The phrase rose unbidden in her mind. She had no idea where she'd heard it or even if she'd recalled it correctly. It definitely wasn't something her father would have said, and her mother...why, she barely remembered her. Regardless of where it came from, it fit this time, this place.

Claire stared into the night. If God *was* in His heaven, could He really hear her from so far away? And, if He could, would He be willing to listen to what she had to say? Or had He crossed her off His list years ago?

Still, what did it hurt to try? Claire knew that even if she walked she'd never be able to sleep if she didn't get what was troubling her off her chest.

The thought of how she'd treated Tony gnawed at her. He'd been nothing but nice to her. She'd been nothing but rotten to him.

Claire took a deep breath and focused on a far-away star.

Dear God, I'm sure You're disappointed in me. I think just about everybody is, my father, Tony, Mrs. Sandy. If You want the truth, which I've heard You do, I'm even a little disappointed in myself. But I want You to know that I'm going to really try to be a better person.

Claire paused and wondered if now would be the appropriate time to ask for a favor. She took a deep breath and plunged ahead.

I know I didn't treat Tony well, but I am sorry and I hope that someway You can let him know that. I'd appreciate it.

Thank You. She hesitated. *Uh, Amen.*

Utterly drained, Claire rested her hand on the rail and took a deep, steadying breath. She'd never before realized how taxing prayer could be. Or how satisfying.

"Claire."

"Tony?" Her heart picked up speed. She turned in the direction of the familiar baritone and strained to see in the darkness. "Where are you?"

"Over here," he said. "On the swing."

She squinted, finally able to make out a dark shape in the shadows. "Can I join you?"

Ordinarily she wouldn't have even asked. But after what had happened earlier she wasn't all that sure how anxious he was to see her.

Tony hesitated. He'd come down to the porch to do some serious thinking. About the well-intentioned lies he'd told. About his future in Millville. And about Claire.

But seeing her now, looking so beautiful in the moonlight, only confused him more. ''I'd like that.''

Claire strolled over. The faint aroma of her plum-scented lotion surrounded her and stirred his senses.

''Have a seat.'' Tony gestured to the empty spot beside him on the swing, wondering why he even bothered. She'd sit where she wanted anyway.

She flashed him an impudent smile. ''Don't mind if I do. Brrr.'' She wrapped her arms across her chest. ''It's chilly out here.''

Tony slanted a gaze sideways, and his lips twitched at her engaging expression. But he made no move to pull her close and he kept his arm firmly at his side rather than slipping it around her shoulders.

He couldn't help being attracted to her, but there were some issues they had to discuss. ''Claire, we need to talk.''

She stiffened beside him, but her voice was offhand when she spoke. ''About what?''

He shifted uncomfortably. "For starters, the ring."

"I'm sorry." Her expression was contrite, but he couldn't be sure if she was sincere or not. "I shouldn't have said anything."

"And I shouldn't have sprung it on you like that," he said. Granted, her comments had stung at the time, but he'd forced himself to remember that this was a woman who shopped at Tiffany's. A woman who demanded perfection. A woman who would never be satisfied with a used diamond from an old woman she'd never met. "I should have been clear that the ring was meant to be a prop, for appearances' sake only."

"Not some gift of the heart," she said softly.

"That's right," Tony said. "Definitely not that."

He'd thought his words would please her, so he was unprepared for the look of disappointment that skittered across her face.

"I acted badly." Claire's gaze remained focused straight ahead, and he couldn't tell what she was thinking. "And I guess I need to know if what happened earlier changes things. Do you still want to go on with this charade?"

Stunned, Tony could only stare. Was this her way of saying goodbye?

"I'd like to continue with it awhile longer," he said slowly. "That is, if you do."

The tightness in her face eased. "I thought you might be giving me the boot."

"Give someone the boot on her birthday?" Tony chuckled. "What kind of guy would do that?"

"I don't know," Claire said. "How 'bout any sane, rational guy? Plus it's after midnight so it's not even my birthday anymore."

Tony stared. This wasn't the Claire he knew. Something was different. He just couldn't quite put his finger on what it was.

"Well, I think I'm sane, and I'm usually rational." He lifted his arm and laid it across the top of the seat, his hand dropping to rest on her shoulder. "And I don't usually give up easily. Besides," he continued, "we had a bet. Remember?"

"A bet?"

"Don't tell me you've forgotten?" He quirked a brow, unable to resist teasing. "Four weeks? You and I? A new record?"

"You really think we could make it?"

Tony let his gaze linger on her beautiful face. "The way I have it figured, we only have three weeks and five days left."

She turned her head slightly and met his gaze. "So, you forgive me?"

"There's nothing to forgive." He reached up with one hand and gently brushed a strand of hair from her face.

Claire moistened her lips with her tongue. "Do you know what I want for my birthday?"

He shook his head, knowing whatever it was he couldn't afford it.

She faced him then, lightly resting her hand on his forearm. "I want to know that you really forgive me. Then I want to kiss and make up."

Tony's gaze dropped to her lips, and he smiled. He might be able to give her what she wanted, after all.

"What do you say, Tony? Does Claire get her wish?"

He wasn't sure who made the first move, but it took just a fraction of a second for her to fall into his arms.

The touch of her lips sent a shock wave through his entire body. Claire returned his kiss as Tony lost himself in the sensation. Finally he raised his mouth from hers.

She murmured a protest and buried her face in his neck, scattering kisses across his warm flesh.

Tony's breath grew ragged.

Claire kissed the pulsing hollow at the base of his throat.

"Claire." Tony grasped her arms and pushed away, the strangled note in his voice letting her know the effort it took.

He raked a hand through his disheveled hair and

blew a harsh breath. "We shouldn't be doing this."

Claire stared in disbelief. When he only shrugged she crossed her arms and flopped back in the swing. With the sudden movement, her robe loosened, exposing the thin silk of her nightie to his view.

His gaze fell to the creamy expanse of her throat.

She jerked the robe together and gave the belt a savage pull. "You're right. It's time to stop."

"It's not that I—"

She closed his lips with the tips of her fingers. "I understand. I know—"

The sound of a car engine stopped her words. She and Tony turned as one to stare down the block, their attention drawn to a sporty-looking older vehicle parked under the corner streetlight.

A car door opened, and someone got out. The door slammed shut even as the sound of laughter filled the evening air.

Tony focused on the faraway figure. It was definitely female.

"Who is that?" Claire said.

"Shh," Tony whispered, and pulled her against the swing. They melted into the darkness. "She's headed this way."

Claire seemed to realize the importance of keeping quiet. Tony could only imagine what would happen if word got out that the new minister was seen in the company of a half-dressed female, fiancée or not.

They sat in silence and waited for the person to pass by. But instead, she turned and sauntered up the front sidewalk. The glow of the yard light reflected off the form. Claire started. Tony sat up straight.

"It's April." He kept his voice so low it was barely audible.

"I thought she was sick," Claire said indignantly. "She could have gotten up at the crack of dawn and cleaned those toilets."

April paused at the door and turned. Claire shrank back in the seat, almost as if she could feel the girl's penetrating gaze.

"Claire? Is that you?"

Claire sighed, and Tony rolled his eyes. Would Claire ever learn to keep her mouth shut?

"We're over here, April," Claire said finally. "Come and join us."

"We? Is Mom with you?" Apprehension ran through the girl's voice, and Tony couldn't keep from smiling. Apparently he and Claire weren't the only ones with something to hide.

The girl moved silently across the wooden floor of the porch. It was almost, Tony thought, as if she knew exactly where every creaky board was located, and avoiding them had become second nature.

"Oh, Tony's with you." April couldn't hide the relief in her voice.

"We're out here enjoying the full moon," Claire said.

Tony stifled a groan.

April's gaze shifted between Tony and Claire, returning to settle on Claire. He knew the girl missed nothing.

"Hello, April." Tony spoke with an easy self-assurance, but he could tell the girl wasn't fooled.

She stood absolutely still, her gaze sharp and assessing. "What are you two doing out in the middle of the night dressed like that?"

Tony's lips twitched. Dressed in a short skirt and a tightly fitted top, the girl had no room to talk. Though Claire might not be fully dressed, her robe covered her more than April's outfit ever could. And though his own sweatpants and T-shirt might not be a fashion statement, they were certainly adequate.

Claire opened her mouth to speak, but Tony grasped her hand and met April's insolent gaze with a direct one of his own.

"Funny you should ask," he said. "I was just about to ask you the same thing."

"I know everyone was disappointed not to see Claire in church this morning." Mrs. Sandy pulled out of the church parking lot and waved to a group of women before shifting her gaze to Tony.

It was the fifth time the woman had made a similar remark, and Tony resisted the urge to point that out. So far he'd bitten his tongue because he knew Mrs. Sandy was only voicing what everyone else thought. They'd all expected Claire to be at his side this morning, but it had been his decision not to wake her.

Last night after April had gone inside, he and Claire had sat in the swing and talked until almost five.

Claire had been surprisingly open. Tony didn't know if it was the lateness of the hour, but once she'd started talking he couldn't shut her up. He'd found out what growing up as Henry Waters's only daughter and heir had been like. And when Claire glossed over her mother's desertion and sidestepped his attempts to ask questions, Tony knew he'd hit a nerve.

By the time they'd headed to their separate rooms, her headache had returned. And he knew that right now, regardless of what Mrs. Sandy or anyone else thought, what Claire needed most was sleep.

"Was April feeling any better this morning?"

Mrs. Sandy had been strangely silent about her

daughter's absence at the church service, only saying the girl was still under the weather.

The light ahead turned red, and Mrs. Sandy slowed the car to a stop. She slanted a sideways glance at Tony, carefully keeping both hands on the wheel. He'd discovered his landlady was a woman who took her driving very seriously.

"I think staying in last night helped April," she said. "Otherwise I have no doubt she would have been out running around half the night and wearing herself to a frazzle."

"Would you have let her go out if she'd asked?" Tony kept his face expressionless.

A teenager crossed against the light, and Mrs. Sandy frowned. Distracted, she shifted a sideways glance at Tony. "Why do you ask?"

"I don't know." Tony forced a chuckle. "Raising a teenager in today's world is difficult. I was just curious."

His answer seemed to satisfy the woman. A rueful expression crossed her face. "I'd say no, but then again April has always had a way of wrapping me around her little finger. So I very well might have let her."

So far, so good. Tony breathed an inward sigh of relief. He hadn't known whether to mention April's little outing last night, but since he knew Mrs. Sandy might have let her go anyway, what would be the point?

''Now, about Claire...''

Tony stifled a groan and leaned back against the seat. The parsonage couldn't be completed too soon.

Claire rolled over in bed and stretched lazily. For the first time in days, the headache that had dogged her every move had vanished. She felt great—wonderful, even.

She smiled, knowing the reason she'd awakened with a completely different attitude.

Tony.

She touched her lips, remembering his kiss, sweet tenderness mixed with a fiery passion that had taken her breath away. But if she wanted to be honest she'd have to admit that was only a small part of the equation. She'd kissed a lot of men in her twenty-eight years, but until Tony, no one had stirred her emotions as he had.

It was too bad he was a minister. If he'd been a businessman interested in relocating to a large city he would be everything she was looking for—he was handsome, fun, and his kisses were dynamite. But Claire a pastor's wife? Even God would have trouble with that one.

Still, it would be nice to make it to the four-week mark and show her father it could be done. And Tony did need her, at least for now. So she'd do best to go with the flow.

The only thing impeding the flow was Mrs. Sandy. If the landlady didn't need her help, everything would be perfect.

Claire slanted a glance at the clock, and her eyes widened. She'd already slept through breakfast and the first part of the lunch shift.

She started to toss off the covers before she stopped herself. Surely Mrs. Sandy would have knocked if she'd needed help? After all, the woman hadn't hesitated to do it yesterday.

Claire snuggled under the covers, a smile tilting the corners of her lips. What was the old saying? No news is good news? She was willing to help, but she'd be stupid to look a gift horse in the mouth.

Thank you, God, for keeping Mrs. Sandy away from me.

Claire's smile widened. She shook her head. Tony was having an influence on her whether he realized it or not.

This was at least the second time since she'd gotten to Millville that she'd prayed.

What did they say? That God worked in mysterious ways? Praying twice in two days? Claire chuckled. It didn't get much stranger than that.

Chapter Eight

Claire glanced at her reddened hands and grimaced. Three weeks of cleaning had clearly taken its toll. The acrylic nails were gone, and the once perfect cuticles had a few jagged edges. Tonight she'd have to slather her hands with that expensive lotion Tony had given her, or replace the word "hands" with "claws."

It had been so sweet of him to think of her on his trip to Des Moines. The scented lotion couldn't have set him back more than ten dollars, but it was the thoughtfulness of the gift that had brought a lump to her throat.

Tony treated her as if she was someone special, and she was beginning to like it. Claire sighed and laid down the toothbrush she was using to clean the grout. Yes, she was really going to miss the guy.

"Hey, gorgeous." Tony's arm slipped around her waist. "What are you doing?"

Claire leaned her head against his chest and inhaled his clean, fresh scent. "Thinking about you."

He turned her in his arms until they faced each other. A knowing glow lit his dark eyes, and that languid warmth that she always felt when he was near flooded her limbs.

"I missed seeing you last night."

"Did you?" She couldn't keep a smile from tipping her lips.

"You bet. I really wish you'd give it a try."

Tony taught a Bible study class on Wednesday nights, and although he'd asked her to come for the past few weeks, Claire had always refused. Since she was going to be leaving soon, she was trying not to get too close to anyone in the congregation. Except for Jocelyn. And of course Dottie.

"Dottie asked us over for dinner Saturday night." Even as she spoke the words they sounded strange against her lips. She knew they shouldn't. Since she'd arrived in Millville, she and Tony had been treated as a couple. Of course, Claire reminded herself that was to be expected. After all, their wedding date was fast approaching.

And approaching equally fast was the day they would split up. They'd stage a big blowup, she'd hurl the ring in his face, and that would be the end of it. She'd finally convinced Tony that breaking up would be a much better way to end the relationship than confessing. Years later, he could tell the elders the truth if he wanted.

"I'm afraid Saturday won't work." Tony shook his head regretfully. "The youth group is having a lock-in at the church, and it's customary for the minister to be a chaperone." He shot her a sideways glance. "I sort of said you'd help, too."

"No. You didn't?"

He smiled that engaging smile she found so hard to resist. "Actually I did."

"A lock-in?"

"C'mon, Claire. It'll be fun."

"Hmm." Claire ran a finger down the side of his cheek and smiled in satisfaction when the muscles tensed beneath her touch. "You and I? Together all night? I'm not so sure that we might not need our own chaperones."

He grasped her fingers with his hand and kissed her palm. "I don't want to burst your bubble but I think twenty freshmen will be more than enough to keep us in line."

"Ya think?" Claire purposely made her voice low and sultry.

"You want to know what I think?" Tony pulled

her close, and his fingers reached up and unclasped her hair clip. Her hair tumbled down like a dark cloud. "I'm glad that right now it's just you and me."

"Me, too." A tingle traveled up Claire's spine, and she brought her arms up then looped them around Tony's neck. "Since we are alone, may I ask what you have in mind, suh?"

Her horrid attempt at a southern accent brought a smile to his face. "Why, Miss Claire—" he mimicked her weak attempt with an equally feeble one of his own "—I had it in my mind to kiss you."

She decided not to remind him that they'd decided it would be best to keep their kisses to a minimum. Instead she fluttered her lashes coquettishly in her best southern belle manner. "Then what, pray tell, are you waiting for?"

He answered immediately, lowering his lips to hers and pulling her tight against him.

Claire's hand rose, and her fingers raked his hair, then gripped his neck like a lifeline as she drowned in his kisses.

His lips moved from her mouth to her neck, and Claire's breath grew ragged. His heart beat fast against her chest.

"And to think we weren't going to do this any more."

The warm kisses behind her ear stopped immediately. Tony stepped back. Claire cursed herself for uttering the words.

She loved being in Tony's arms, loved kissing him, loved the closeness. They both knew it wasn't going to last. But for now, for her, the closeness was enough.

She knew Tony worried that the kisses would lead to something more. But even if she was willing to throw caution, not to mention morals, to the wind, Tony was not. He'd made it very clear the other night that he practiced what he preached. True intimacy was reserved for the marriage bed.

She'd surprised him when she'd agreed. Though she may have built a reputation as a love 'em and leave 'em kind of gal, the truth was she'd left a lot of them, and she hadn't loved any of them.

Oh, at one time she'd thought she was in love. She'd even tried to break up the man's engagement. But later she'd realized the only reason she wanted him was that she couldn't have him.

She studied Tony's handsome face. Was that why she was so attracted to him? Because he could never be hers?

"I'm sorry, Claire." Tony's voice was husky and filled with regret. "We said we'd keep our distance. It's just that you looked so beautiful."

She had to laugh. God forgive her, she did. She'd borrowed a pair of April's jean shorts, shorts more suited to the girl's gangly thinness than

Claire's womanly curves. And the little cotton T-shirt with Millville Monarchs across the back and a tiny butterfly on the front just above one breast couldn't have been more hideous. Certainly it didn't compare to the trendy designer outfits she was used to wearing.

If only Daddy could see me now.

Claire's smile widened. "I think you need to try that line on somebody who would buy it."

"You do look beautiful." His gaze didn't waver.

Confused, Claire looked away. She realized with a start that Tony meant what he'd said.

It was unbelievable. She'd had men compliment her when she was wearing a thousand-dollar dress or when they wanted something from her, but no one had ever been as sincere as Tony was now.

"Claire?" His probing voice interrupted her thoughts.

She shifted her gaze to meet his.

"Will you?"

She swallowed hard. "Will I what?"

"Will you be a chaperone for the lock-in?"

Disappointment flooded her. She wasn't sure what she'd expected him to ask, but it definitely wasn't that. Claire forced a smile, and when she did speak she was proud her voice gave no clue to her churning emotions. "Sure, why not? It might be fun."

She hadn't spent much time around teenagers. Hadn't really wanted to, if the truth be known. But there were only twenty of them. And they were young. How hard could it be?

"I said no." Claire crossed her arms and leaned against the door.

"C'mon, Miss Waters. Me and Angie here—" the girl gestured to her friend, a petite redhead with wispy hair "—we need some fresh air."

"No."

"I…I get claustrophobic. I think I feel an attack coming on right now."

Claire raised a brow. Next thing Tina would be trying to tell her she had some condition protected by the Americans with Disabilities Act. Goodness knows she'd tried every other excuse in the book. But Claire, who'd acquired the task of monitoring one of the outside exits, had been a surprisingly stern taskmaster. Mainly because she suspected that Tina's desire to go outside was directly tied to the rumble of a motorcycle she'd heard pass by the church off and on tonight. Plus she knew all the tricks. She'd used them herself at that age.

"I'm sure you'll be fine." She'd wasted enough breath trying to explain why no one could leave and she refused to revisit that territory.

Claire gestured with one hand to two boys sitting on the floor playing a board game. "Why don't you go over there? I'm sure they'd love to have you girls join them.''

The redhead rolled her eyes, and Tina let loose a very unladylike snort. ''Get real. Nate and Kendall are the biggest geeks in school.''

Claire fixed her gaze on the girl but didn't respond.

''I know we're in a church and all but don't go getting all pious on me.'' Tina tossed a strand of honey-colored hair over her shoulder. ''I bet you never hung out with losers when you were our age.''

The girl didn't wait for an answer. With a smug smile she grabbed her friend's arm, turned and headed over to where a large group of teens sat watching a movie.

''What was that all about?'' Tony said, coming up beside her.

Claire shrugged. ''I suggested the girls might want to join Nate and Kendall, but they promptly nixed that idea. Said they didn't want to be seen associating with losers.''

''Did you call them on that?'' Tony's voice was taut with an emotion Claire couldn't identify.

''I tried to.'' She met his skeptical gaze, but her tone sounded defensive even to her own ears. ''But they just said something to the effect that they knew if I was their age I wouldn't have been caught dead hanging out with the geeks, either.''

"And what did you say to that?"

"I didn't say anything," Claire said. "What could I say? It was the truth."

"Oh, Claire." Tony chuckled. "All I can say is you obviously didn't know what you were missing."

Claire raised a brow.

"I'm serious." Tony spoke without embarrassment. "I was a geek in high school."

"Yeah, right," Claire scoffed. Tony was way too gorgeous to have ever been anything but a hunk.

"Well, I was." His voice was matter-of-fact. "Now aren't you glad?"

"Glad?" Her brow furrowed in confusion.

"That you met me now." He laughed and gave her a wink. "Because back then I would have been one of those geeks you avoided. And you have to admit it would have been your loss."

Claire couldn't help but laugh with him. And strange as it may sound, she had to agree. It really would have been her loss.

Tony rolled the dice and automatically counted off the number of spaces, his mind everywhere but on the game.

He glanced across the room, his gaze settling on Claire. She looked lovely. The pale green of the cotton sheath accentuated her tan, and her hair flowed down around her shoulders in loose waves just the way he liked it.

Claire caught his eye and lifted one hand, wiggling her fingers in hello. He smiled, then quickly returned his attention to the game he was playing with Nate and Kendall.

"Your fiancée is beautiful," Nate said with something akin to awe in his voice.

"Yeah," Kendall echoed. "Real pretty. You're lucky. Those kind never give us a chance."

"You know, guys, I hate to say this," Tony said with a smile. "But when I was your age they didn't like me, either."

He'd had everything going against him then. He'd been short. He hadn't really shot up until he'd been close to eighteen. And he'd been fat.

It had been hard moving so much. Some kids made friends easily. Tony's friends had been the ice cream carton and the television. Braces and glasses had pushed him over the edge into a land where, pretty girls aside, he was lucky anyone talked to him. At least Nate and Kendall had each other.

And he had Claire. A woman who ten years ago wouldn't have given him the time of day.

"Pastor?"

Tony lifted his gaze and realized that the boys must have been talking while he was reliving the past.

"Yes, Nate?"

"So what happened? What changed?"

"Actually..." Tony's gaze shifted between the boys, and he decided if his story could help these two, it would be worth dredging up the past. Those days were long behind him and he rarely looked back, but it was important the boys realized that high school was just a small part of anyone's life. He took a deep breath and continued. "When I was your age, I hardly had any friends. In fact..."

Across the room Claire watched Tony. She didn't know what he was saying, but it looked serious. The dice and game board sat untouched in front of the three, and the boys' faces were riveted to the young minister.

Her gaze shifted to Nate and Kendall. Judging by the clothes they wore, the two had not one ounce of fashion sense, and whoever cut their hair obviously chose not to keep up on the latest styles. Still, there was something in their faces that made her pause. That made her not dismiss them as easily as she would in the past.

Maybe because now she was old enough to see the youthful innocence behind the blemishes. Maybe it was because she'd taken the time to talk to the boys earlier and found they both had a sense of humor in sync with her own. Or maybe, just maybe, being around Tony was good for her.

Claire shook her head and took a deep breath.

Where was all this sentimental stuff coming from? The way she was going the next thing you knew she'd be canceling her subscription to her fashion magazines and wearing jeans and sweatshirts. In public. And maybe she wouldn't even care that her diamond had flaws.

Why didn't that thought send chills up her spine as it once had? She wasn't a Pollyanna, by any means, and although this time in Millville and Tony's influence might cause her to rethink a few things, who she was deep down would never change.

Claire scanned the crowd. There wasn't anyone here with that power.

Her gaze settled on Tony.

Or was there?

Tony headed down the running path that circled the outskirts of Millville. The rhythmic beat of his shoes against the asphalt soothed his jangled nerves.

It had been a bad couple of days, and he needed to work off the stress. He'd decided after the lock-in to confess to the church elders and hope for the best. But he'd had difficulty arranging a meeting, and then Kendall had stopped by the church to talk.

After speaking with the boy Tony realized he couldn't take the chance that the elders would tell him he had to leave. He knew Kendall had recently moved to Millville, but until yesterday he hadn't understood how hard that had been on the teen.

A connection had been forged the night he'd shared his story with Nate and Kendall. It was as if God had sent him here to minister to these boys knowing Tony was someone who truly understood the pressures they faced.

So he'd kept his mouth shut.

Claire had taken the news in stride that the engagement would continue for a while longer. She seemed oddly content with the status quo. Tony decided it must mean, since her father hadn't shown any signs of softening, she really had nowhere else to go. And, although Mrs. Sandy still had to wake her up at times, Claire had fit into the household with surprising ease.

Claire.

They were tied together in an arrangement that would soon end. While it was becoming clearer why he'd been sent to Millville, the reason Claire had been thrown into the equation was more difficult to understand.

Despite their physical attraction to each other, Claire and he were too different for any long-term commitment. They both knew that.

Of course, he had to admit that they'd gotten along pretty well, considering those differences.

He smiled. Claire always kept him guessing. He never knew what she'd say next. And when she fluttered those long black eyelashes and her full lips turned upward in that dazzling smile, there wasn't anything Tony wouldn't do for her.

He wished he could say she'd do the same for him. Although she attended church every Sunday, she seemed to focus more on the social aspect than the spiritual. And although Dottie had asked Claire repeatedly to go to Bible study with her, she still hadn't agreed to give it a try.

Tony knew everyone wondered why his fiancée wasn't more involved with the church. Personally he didn't care how it looked, he just wished she had a stronger faith. Because if she didn't get turned on to God living in the same house with a minister, would she ever?

But when had that minister ever witnessed to her?

The realization hit Tony like a lightning bolt, and he stopped, stunned. He'd pondered Claire's lack of faith. He'd prayed for her. But he'd never sat down and simply shared what God meant to him.

A deep sense of shame filled him.

"Are you okay?"

Tony's gaze jerked in the direction of the voice. A slender young woman about his own age, dressed in running shorts and a T-shirt, jogged in place, a worried look on her face.

Tony paused and thought how he'd let Claire

down. "No." He shook his head. He'd paid more attention to Claire's body than her soul. "I'm not okay."

"Do you need a doctor?"

He frowned. "Why would I need a doctor?"

A flush of red shot up the woman's neck.

"You stopped so suddenly and then you just stood there," she stammered. "I was concerned something might be wrong."

The woman shifted uncomfortably, and once again Tony cursed himself. Couldn't he do anything right? There'd been no reason to be so abrupt.

"I'm sorry." He flashed her an apologetic smile. "I got to thinking and—"

"That's fine." She nervously fiddled with a loose thread on her shorts. "You don't have to explain."

He could sense her unease. Although not unattractive, he instinctively knew that unlike Claire, this woman wasn't comfortable talking to men she didn't know. The knowledge that she'd stopped to help anyway made Tony go out of his way to be extra nice.

"I don't believe we've met." He extended his hand. "I'm Tony Karelli, the new pastor at Grace Community."

"Rachel Tanner." Her whole face lit up when she smiled, and Tony realized she was prettier than he'd first thought. "I'm a member of your church. Or at least I was when I lived in Millville before. I just moved back, and I'm looking forward to getting involved again."

Tony smiled. It was so refreshing to find someone interested in volunteering.

"Welcome back, Rachel," he said softly. "I know lots of committees that could use your help. And your husband? Is he interested in becoming involved, too?"

"I'm not married," she said quickly. Her gaze dropped to the ground, and she brushed back a strand of blond hair that had come loose from her ponytail.

"What a coincidence," Tony said, trying to lighten the moment and ease her embarrassment. "Neither am I."

It was the wrong thing to say. Her gaze lifted, and a spark of interest flickered in her soft blue eyes.

Tony groaned to himself. It was true he wasn't married, but he *was* supposed to be engaged. But how could he tell her that now? It would look as if he thought she was interested in him and that he was trying to warn her off. Talk about embarrassing the woman. Besides, in a couple of weeks Claire *would* be gone.

The pretending would be over, and he would be free to move on with his life. Maybe he'd find himself a nice woman—someone like Rachel Tanner perhaps—who was from Millville and wanted to live here, someone who went to church because she wanted to, not because she had to.

He knew he should feel relieved. But all the way home, instead of thinking about a slender blonde with blue eyes, all he could see was a raven-haired beauty with eyes as dark as night.

Tony sighed. If he didn't know better, he'd have to wonder if he just might not be falling in love with the one woman in the world who was all wrong for him.

Chapter Nine

Claire's head jerked up at the knock on her bedroom door.

"Claire, it's time to go."

She smiled at the familiar baritone and covered the receiver with her hand. "I'll be ready in five minutes," she yelled at the door. "I'll meet you downstairs."

She waited until she heard Tony walk away before she turned her attention back to the phone.

"Daddy, I'm going to have to let you go." She lowered her voice even though there was no one else in the room. "No, I don't need any money. I told you I'm doing fine."

But Henry Waters was used to controlling a conversation, and he kept talking until Claire had no choice but to cut him off.

"Daddy, I'm going to hang up now. Yes, I'll call you tomorrow. And yes, this time I'll call collect. Love you, too. Bye."

She hung up the phone and sat there, still amazed that her father had come around so quickly. Three weeks after he'd more or less told her never to darken his door again he'd done a complete about-face. Once again she was his darling daughter, his little princess.

Claire wasn't sure what had impressed him more, that she and Tony were still together or that she had a job and was making it on her own. Of course, she'd had to fudge a little about the job. He'd never have believed she was a maid, so she'd found it necessary to embellish the position.

When she thought about it, director of catering really wasn't that big a stretch. After all, she did cater to the guests. What else did you call it when you refilled their coffee and got them extra napkins?

The clock in the hall chimed and Claire rose, casting one last look in the mirror before heading out the door and down the stairs. She knew she should let Tony know that she and her father had reconciled, but she was afraid he'd do the noble thing and send her packing.

She wanted the time to be right for him, wanted his position to be secure. Over the past weeks she'd come to believe this town and this church needed Tony Karelli. And Claire was committed to doing whatever she could to insure he could stay.

If that meant staying here longer, so be it. Anyway, she really wasn't ready to leave Millville yet. Or Tony.

Claire found Tony at the dining room table, a newspaper in one hand and a cup of coffee in the other. She stopped in the doorway and watched him silently for a few seconds.

The morning light streamed in through the window and shone on his dark hair like a halo. Today he'd worn her favorite Abercrombie shirt, a burgundy cotton with a navy stripe across the front. He was so incredibly handsome. And so very wonderful. Claire's chest tightened. How was she ever going to let him go?

Get a hold of yourself. She gave herself a mental shake, strode into the room and kicked the leg of his chair.

"Hey, what's that you're drinking?" Claire crossed her arms across her chest and looked pointedly at the half empty cup in his hand.

"Mrs. Sandy's generic blend." Tony made a face and set the mug down. "I'm getting primed for the good stuff."

Claire smiled. "The Grateful Bread's Costa Rican blend?"

Tony returned her smile and pushed the mug aside. "I can almost smell it now."

"What about the pecan streusel coffee cake?" Claire teased.

The Grateful Bread café bakery had different daily specials, and she and Tony had quickly become addicted to the Wednesday feature, a buttery rich coffee cake loaded with pecans.

"That, too." Tony grinned and pulled her onto his lap. He nuzzled her neck. "Hmm. Maybe I'm just hungry, but you smell delicious."

"It's the lotion you bought me." A shiver traveled up Claire's spine. With a deliberate motion she tilted her face toward him, and when she spoke next to his ear her voice was nothing more than a husky whisper. "You're the one who smells good." Her lips brushed his. "Mmm. You taste good, too."

His eyes darkened and his arms tightened around her. She held her breath.

The door leading to the kitchen flew open. "Now April, I want you—"

Mrs. Sandy stopped. April bumped into her from behind. The landlady's hand rose to her lips, her mouth forming a perfect O.

Tony jerked back, and even though Claire didn't want to, she hopped off his lap.

"I'm so sorry, Pastor." A blotch of red darkened the woman's cheeks. "I didn't know you and Claire were still here."

"We got a late start this morning," Tony said, looking a little flustered.

"Or an early one," April offered, smiling innocently. "Depends on how you look at it, I guess."

"April!" Mrs. Sandy shot her daughter a warning glance before she turned her attention to Claire and Tony. "You know, if you have a few minutes, this might be a good chance to discuss your wedding reception. I assume you'll want to have—"

"How 'bout we talk about that later?" Tony stood and grabbed Claire's hand. "Claire and I have to run. That coffee cake always goes quickly."

Though it was only an excuse, it was a good one. Everyone in town knew if you didn't have a piece on your plate by ten-thirty, you might as well forget it. But Claire knew that wasn't the real reason Tony wanted to rush off. For the past week, Mrs. Sandy had repeatedly tried to corner them about their wedding plans. Even when they told her last week it was only going to be a small ceremony with immediate family and close friends, Mrs. Sandy wasn't appeased. She insisted whether it was fifty people or five hundred, you still needed to plan ahead.

"We're going to have to sit down and talk about this soon."

Tony smiled and Claire waved a quick goodbye. When the door fell shut behind them, Claire heaved a sigh of relief. They walked in silence down the shaded sidewalk toward downtown. Mrs. Sandy's words had once again brought to the forefront a fact that neither one of them seemed to want to face. Their time together was finite. And soon it would be over.

"Did I tell you I'm going to Bible study tonight?" Claire said in a deliberately offhand manner.

Tony stopped in his tracks. "What did you say?"

"I'm going to Bible study tonight." The look of shock on his face pleased her, and for once she didn't mind repeating herself.

"You never told me you were even *considering* going. I believe the last time we discussed it, your exact words were 'no way.'"

Her lips twitched. He'd recalled that part perfectly. "What can I say?" She shrugged. "I'm a woman. We change our minds."

"But why? Not that I'm not happy about it—I am," he hastened to reassure her, "but it's just so out of the blue."

"Not so sudden," Claire said. "I've been thinking about it for several days."

Actually she'd been thinking about it ever since Dottie told her she was hosting the activity and begged Claire to come. But, she reminded herself, she wasn't going simply because it was at Dottie's home. Listening to Tony's sermons the last few weeks had piqued her interest in learning more about the Bible. So, attending Bible study at her friend's house would serve two purposes—make Dottie happy and give Claire the opportunity to learn a little more about God. Maybe she'd even be able to get the inside scoop on His plans for her life.

"I can't tell you how happy that makes me." Tony took her hand and gave it a squeeze.

She smiled at him, and they walked the rest of the way with her hand clasped loosely in his. A strange sense of contentment stole over Claire, and she wondered if she would ever again feel this happy.

Their corner booth was waiting and the waitress didn't even ask what they wanted. It was the same every week. A couple of people from church stopped by to visit, and it wasn't until they were on their second cup of coffee that she and Tony were finally alone.

Claire added another packet of sugar to the strong brew and took a sip. "I heard you pacing the floor last night. Something bothering you?"

Tony set his cup down and paused, a thoughtful

expression on his face. "I was having trouble with this week's sermon. I needed a few examples for some points I was making. It was the strangest thing. I'd sleep for a while, then I'd wake up thinking of an example and have to write it down before I forgot it." He laughed. "I know it sounds crazy."

"Not so crazy. That used to happen to me a lot when I worked in advertising." Claire remembered all too well those sleepless nights. "How's it coming now?"

"Better." His hands cupped his mug and he nodded. "Actually I think it might be one of my best."

"Your sermons are all good," Claire said. "They really make a person think."

"Thank you, Claire." Tony gazed at her as if he'd never seen her before. "I appreciate that."

"I'm not saying it to be nice." Claire shrugged. "It's the truth."

"Heaven forbid you should say it to be nice." Tony's lips quirked upward, and a teasing glint filled his dark eyes.

"You'd better watch yourself, Tony Karelli." Claire leaned across the table, a melodramatic warning in her tone. "You know what your teasing does to me."

"Makes you mad?" he said with an impish grin.

"Something like that." She glanced at him

through lowered lashes, unable to keep a tiny smile from tugging at her lips. "Actually it makes me want to kiss you."

His grin widened, and he tossed a couple of bills on the table. "C'mon." He grabbed Claire's hand. "Let's get out of here. I want to hear more about this. Maybe I can even use it in a sermon sometime."

"Are you teasing me again, Tony?" Claire slid out of the booth and followed him out of the café.

"I hope so." He chuckled. "That's my intention."

They took the long way home through the park. Claire was surprised she didn't see anyone she knew. Tony just smiled and claimed that he'd paid them all to leave. She couldn't resist. She kissed him. And then, when he laughed, she kissed him again. Her lips were still tingling when they reached the bed-and-breakfast.

"I'm going to have to run." Tony ran his thumb lightly over the back of her hand. "I'm already late for a meeting."

Claire watched him drive away before heading into the house. She hummed a little love song that had been on the radio when she woke up, its upbeat tempo matching her mood.

"My mom's looking for you." Like a splash of cold water, April's voice brought Claire back to reality.

"Did she say why?" Claire raised a brow.

"I dunno. I didn't ask. Not my business." Something in the girl's eyes told Claire she knew more than she was saying.

"You must have some idea." Claire pinned the girl with a sharp gaze.

April shrugged. "It's probably about that wedding reception she's catering Friday. Her helper backed out on her this morning, and I think she's looking for an extra pair of hands."

Friday night? Claire groaned.

"Why can't you help?" Claire said bluntly. "Your hands look perfectly capable to me."

"Because." April smiled smugly. "My hands will be with me in Des Moines that night. Me and my friends have tickets to Froggy Way."

Even though she and Tony didn't have plans yet for Friday night, she knew they'd probably go out. After all, how many more Friday nights did they have left? "I'm sure there's someone else that could help."

"Yeah, right." April snorted. "Do you think she'd be asking you if there were?"

"What do you mean by that?"

"Just what it sounds like." April met her gaze. "What are you going to do, make her beg?"

"Beg?" A lump formed in the pit of Claire's stomach.

"Well, you're not really the volunteering kind."

April laughed, a harsh, unpleasant sound. "You act like it's such a big deal when you do any little thing."

"So do you." The childish reply slipped past Claire's lips.

"But I'm her daughter." The girl's voice rang with the arrogance of youth. "You're a guest who's living here rent free. If you weren't Pastor's fiancée you'd be long gone."

The lump in Claire's stomach turned rock hard, and for some reason it affected her ability to breathe normally. "Did your mother say that?"

April had the grace to look slightly abashed. "She might not have said it. But I can't imagine why she'd put up with you for any other reason."

"Tell me, April. What bothers you most? The fact that no guy has given you a second glance since I moved in? Or that your mother's finally expecting you to shoulder some of the responsibility?"

April stepped back as if she'd been slapped, and her blue eyes turned frosty. One of her comments, Claire wasn't sure which, had definitely struck a nerve.

Good. Maybe now you know how I feel.

It wasn't a very charitable thought, but Claire wasn't feeling particularly charitable. April's words had hurt. Even more because some of what the girl had said was true.

Although Claire's competitive spirit wouldn't allow her to do shoddy work, she certainly hadn't put forth top effort. And April was right. She never volunteered to do more. But surely the woman wasn't just keeping her on because she didn't want to offend Tony. If that was the case, Claire would have to leave. She'd never been one to overstay her welcome.

But Mrs. Sandy had taken her in when she was penniless and had nowhere else to go. Hurt feelings aside, if the woman needed her help, how could she walk out on her now?

Footsteps sounded in the hall, and suddenly Claire was face-to-face with Mrs. Sandy.

"Why, Claire, I didn't expect you back so early."

"Tony had a meeting at the church." Thankfully her voice didn't betray her churning emotions.

"April, could you go check on the laundry?" Mrs. Sandy smiled at her daughter. "I'd like to talk to Claire privately."

"Sure, glad to help." April smiled sweetly, slanting a sideways glance at Claire.

"Is something wrong?" Claire said the moment April left the room.

"Don't look so solemn." Mrs. Sandy laughed and wrapped her arm around Claire, giving her shoulder a squeeze. "It's nothing serious. Did you and Tony have a nice time this morning?"

"We did," Claire said, remembering the coffee cake and the kisses.

"I don't suppose after all that coffee I could interest you in some tea?"

Claire shook her head. "None for me, thanks."

She followed Mrs. Sandy into the kitchen and took a seat at the table. Apprehension coursed through her veins, and Claire wished the woman would just say what she had to say and be done with it.

But Mrs. Sandy seemed in no hurry. The landlady busied herself pouring a glass of tea from the refrigerator. Not until she had added a couple of ice cubes and wiped the counter free of water spots did she finally pull out a chair and sit down.

"I'm just going to go ahead and say this." Mrs. Sandy's expression stilled and grew serious. "I've got a business proposition for you."

Claire stared, speechless. Whatever she'd expected, it wasn't this. "A business proposition?"

Mrs. Sandy plopped a cube of sugar into her glass and stirred it into the tea with her spoon. "I don't know if I've told you, but I supplement my income by doing some catering on the side."

"What kind of catering?" When Claire had worked for her father, one of her duties had been to make the arrangements for all his corporate parties.

"I've pretty much limited myself to wedding receptions, anniversary and graduation parties." Mrs. Sandy took a sip of the tea and set it on the table. "But lately I've been getting more calls for dinner parties and business events."

Claire marveled at the woman's stamina. She would have thought owning the bed-and-breakfast and raising a teenage daughter would have been more than enough for anyone. "Sounds like you've got a good thing going."

"I do, but..." Mrs. Sandy leaned forward, moving her tea aside. "I'd like to expand. That's why I wanted to talk to you. I think you're just the person I've been looking for."

"Me?" Claire couldn't have been more surprised. Mrs. Sandy knew she couldn't cook. They laughed about it often. "How could I help you?"

Mrs. Sandy raised a hand. "Before we go any further, I want us to be clear on one thing. I'm not asking you to help me. I want you to be my partner."

"You're kidding." Claire was totally confused. "Aren't you?"

Laughter flowed from Mrs. Sandy's lips, and she patted Claire's hand. "Oh, my dear, I'm so bad at this."

Claire smiled.

"The catering has helped me make ends meet since my husband died. The problem is, with running this place I'm limited to when I can go out and meet with the clients and get everything arranged. Doing it over the phone doesn't cut it."

"So where would I come in?" In spite of knowing she wouldn't be around long enough to see this project through to fruition, Claire couldn't help the adrenaline surge.

"You'd do everything else from meeting with the clients to coordinating the display of the food." Mrs. Sandy eyes sparkled. "I'd do the majority of the cooking and baking."

Ideas tumbled fast and furious through Claire's brain. She'd always loved throwing elaborate parties. This wouldn't even seem like work.

"I know that as a minister's wife, you'll have certain responsibilities," Mrs. Sandy said. "But we can work around those."

Minister's wife.

Her heart plummeted. In the rush of excitement she'd forgotten one important fact. She'd be leaving soon. But Mrs. Sandy had done so much for her already, and this was a great opportunity. How could she just turn her down flat?

"Let me think about it," Claire said, trying to act as if she didn't notice the disappointment in Mrs. Sandy's eyes. "In the meantime, April said you have a function Friday night you might need some help with.''

Mrs. Sandy nodded. ''The Johnson-Kinisaw reception.''

''Okay, how about if I volunteer to help and we see what kind of team we make?''

''Sounds like a plan,'' the woman said immediately.

Claire hated herself for putting the hope back in the landlady's eyes, but she wanted to repay Mrs. Sandy for her kindness, and helping her out until she left seemed the best way to do that.

''But I'd like to ask a little favor of you.''

''Sure, anything.'' Mrs. Sandy didn't even qualify her answer.

''Don't say yes so quickly,'' Claire warned. ''Because this is a big one.''

''What is it?''

''I want you to teach me to cook.''

''How is it?''

Tony had barely taken a bite of the biscuit before Claire was in his face, her eyes sparkling like black diamonds.

He paused. Never before had she been concerned about the food he ate, but then again never had he tasted a biscuit like this one. He chewed slowly, forced a chunk down his throat, then washed it down with a big drink of water. "Good."

"Claire made them herself," Mrs. Sandy said proudly.

Now it all made sense. The two women giggling in the kitchen before the meal. Claire's anxious look when he'd taken a biscuit and it had slipped from his fingers and dropped to the plate with a resounding plunk.

"They're great-looking biscuits," he said glancing at the overflowing basket.

The biscuits were a perfect example of how looks could be deceiving. Golden brown, they could easily have been an advertisement for baking powder biscuits as good as Grandma used to make. Unfortunately they tasted like Grandma had made them herself…fifty years ago.

Tony wondered what had made Claire try her hand at baking. Like anyone, he enjoyed good food. But his mother had been a career woman, and the only time he'd had home cooking was when he'd spent time at his grandmother's or when the cook was in her down-home cooking phase.

If Claire thought he expected her to be another Martha Stewart, she was mistaken. He didn't have any such expectations for his wife….

Tony brought himself up short. This was getting out of hand. He'd started to believe his own lies.

And the startling thing was, he found himself wishing they weren't lies.

Why couldn't it happen?

His heart picked up speed at the thought. He and Claire? Together forever? Could it possibly happen?

He had some serious thinking to do. And he was going to need his energy. Tony smiled at Claire and held out his hand for the bread basket. "Could you pass me another biscuit, please? They're delicious."

Chapter Ten

❧

Claire sat back in the chair and took a sip of the apricot tea. Crisp and cool, it soothed her parched throat. Her friend was indeed the consummate hostess.

Tonight, Dottie's smile just wouldn't quit. The Bible study had been a complete success. Despite the fact that it was a beautiful evening, attendance had been good. Claire glanced around the room and counted ten women who'd stayed for the social hour and refreshments.

"I'm glad you stuck around." Jocelyn pulled up a chair next to Claire. "We haven't talked in forever."

Claire smiled. As she recalled, she and Jocelyn had gone shopping and had lunch together just two days before. "I'm sorry I was late."

"You didn't miss anything." Jocelyn brushed back a strand of hair, and Claire couldn't help but admire her friend's nails. She resisted the urge to glance at her own less than perfect ones. "Unless you were dying to hear everyone talk about their kids. I, of course, found the part about potty training positively riveting."

The light sarcasm in her friend's voice came through loud and clear, and once again Claire had to smile.

"I tried to save you a seat by me, but Rachel snagged it at the last minute," Jocelyn continued.

"Rachel?" Claire assumed Jocelyn was talking about the woman who had sat on her right. "The blonde?"

Jocelyn nodded.

"Do I know her?"

Her friend paused and thought for a minute. "I don't think so. She just moved back to Millville, although she wasn't gone that long. Maybe six months or so."

"She seems nice," Claire said grudgingly. It wasn't very Christian of her, but Claire couldn't help wanting to find fault with Rachel. Maybe it was because the blonde fit in so well with the group and Claire felt like an outsider. Whatever the reason, she shifted her gaze and studied the woman with a critical eye.

Rachel was pretty enough, if you liked that

blond-haired, blue-eyed farmer's daughter type. Personally, Claire found that wholesome look tiresome. Especially when it wasn't well done.

The woman's shoulder-length hair needed a good undercut while her brows screamed to be shaped. Her dress at least was adequate. Claire had a similar one hanging in her closet, and it was one of her favorites. But Rachel was built differently than Claire, so the style wasn't nearly as flattering on the blonde.

"What are you smiling about?" Jocelyn leaned forward, her eyes bright with interest.

For a second, Claire thought about telling her. A month ago she wouldn't have hesitated. But listening to Tony's sermons all these weeks had apparently had an impact.

Claire shook her head, unable to believe she was being this good. Before long she wouldn't even recognize herself. "I guess you're just going to have to call me Pollyanna."

"What?" Confusion clouded Jocelyn's gaze. "Call you who?"

Claire laughed. "Forget it." She set her glass on a coaster. "Tell me what you have planned for Saturday."

"I'm so excited." Jocelyn's face brightened. "We're going to have so much fun."

"What's on the agenda?"

"Cards."

Claire's smile froze. A card party? Was she serious?

"Look, I know it sounds corny but it's the best I can do here. Besides, Adam thinks it'll be great fun. And that's not all." Jocelyn paused dramatically. "After we finish with cards, we're going to do a pie exchange."

"Yeah, right." Claire rolled her eyes.

"I'm serious."

"Uh-huh." Claire shook her head. Did her friend really think she'd believe that? "Next you'll be telling me we're going to follow that with a rousing game of bingo."

Jocelyn chuckled. "When you say it that way it does sound ridiculous. But remember this is Millville, Iowa."

"Thanks for the reminder." Claire smiled ruefully. "Okay, so tell me, what is a pie exchange?"

"You can't laugh."

Claire crossed her fingers and smiled.

"And try to keep an open mind." Jocelyn took a sip of her tea. "What happens is all the women bring a different kind of pie to the party. At the end of the evening, we cut them into small slices so everybody can try at least two or three kinds."

Claire raised a brow. "Sounds...interesting."

"It took me a while to get used to it, too," Jocelyn said with a smile. "But it's the thing to do. Isn't that right, Rachel?"

Claire didn't realize Rachel had come over. The blonde pulled up a chair and sat, apparently deciding Jocelyn's question gave her an excuse to join the group. "Isn't what right?"

"I was telling Claire that everyone has a pie exchange when they throw a party," Jocelyn said.

"She's right." Rachel smiled at Claire, her voice soft and pleasant. "Of course, I love pie."

Claire glanced from Rachel to Jocelyn, unable to believe they were actually at a party, discussing something as mundane as pie.

"Rachel is a terrific cook," Jocelyn told Claire. "Wait until you taste her sour cream peach. She always gets a purple ribbon at the state fair. It's incredible."

Dottie pulled up a chair and sat down. "What are you three talking about?"

"Nothing." Claire smiled brightly at Dottie.

"We're talking about what a great cook Rachel is," Jocelyn said. "She's almost as good as Mrs. Sandy."

Claire stifled a groan.

"I heard Mrs. Sandy might be expanding her catering business." Jocelyn looked at Rachel. "You should see if she needs help. With your skills you'd be perfect."

Indignation coursed through Claire, and it was all she could do not to blurt out that *she* was the one who would be helping Mrs. Sandy. That it was *her* skills the woman needed. Only the realization that she was also the one who would be soon gone stopped her.

"I might talk to her about that," Rachel said. "Is she coming Saturday?"

"No." Jocelyn shook her head. "She had other plans."

"Who is coming?" Rachel asked.

"Let's see." Jocelyn thought for a moment. "Besides Adam and me, there's you, Dottie, Tom, Claire, Tony—"

"Tony?" Rachel interrupted.

"Tony Karelli. He's the new minister." Jocelyn smiled at Claire. "You haven't met him yet. He's Cl—"

"Oh, but I have met him," Rachel said. "I was out jogging today, and we sort of ran into each other. Now that is one good-looking man."

"He's adorable." Jocelyn gave Claire a wink. "What do you think, Claire? Is Tony cute?"

"He's okay." Claire stifled a smile. Wait until she told Tony what they'd talked about in Bible study.

"He said he wasn't married," Rachel said. "And I got the distinct impression he might be interested in me. Do you know if he's dating anyone?"

Rachel's expectant gaze shifted around the

group, and an empathetic pain stabbed Claire's heart. The woman really didn't know the score.

"He said he wasn't married?" Claire asked, more to fill the awkward silence than to continue the conversation. "Did he say anything about being engaged?"

"No." Rachel's brow furrowed, and she shook her head. "He led me to believe he was unattached. Even said he was looking forward to seeing me in church on Sunday."

"That's Tony for you," Dottie said with a nervous laugh, picking at a piece of lint on her pants. "He's so personable, he makes everyone feel special."

"That's right," Jocelyn seconded loyally. "He's one guy that can make you feel like you're the only woman in the room. I had the same impression the first time I met him."

Although Claire didn't believe a word of it, she appreciated their efforts.

"So you're saying he's engaged?" Even if they wouldn't have heard the disappointment in her tone, the expression on her face said it all.

The three slowly nodded in unison.

"But to who?"

Jocelyn nudged Claire. "Show her your ring."

"Your ring?" A sick look crossed the blonde's face, and a bolt of red shot up her neck.

"Tony and I are engaged, Rachel." Claire held

up her left hand. "In fact, we're getting married in two weeks."

"I found the perfect woman for you."

"Another woman?" Tony screwed a new light bulb into the chandelier and smiled at her. The dimple in his cheek flashed, and her heart melted. "No, thanks. One is more than I can handle."

"Don't you even want to know who she is?"

"Nope." He climbed down the ladder and pulled it shut, resting it against the wall. "Not interested."

"She's pretty." If you like blondes.

"In case you haven't heard—" he spoke so low she had to move closer to hear "—I already have a fiancée. And she's *beautiful*."

"But she won't be around forever," Claire said. "What are you going to do when she's gone?"

"I don't know." He paused, and his face clouded for a second. "I don't want to even think about that now."

Ask me to stay.

Tony stared so intently, for an instant Claire feared she'd spoken her wish aloud.

"Last night at Bible study, Rachel Tanner said she had the hots for you."

Tony rolled his eyes. "Yeah, right."

"She did." Claire couldn't resist pushing the point. "Rachel thinks you're cute."

"The woman has good taste." Tony grinned. "I'll give her that."

"So you like her?"

"Claire, give me a break. I just met her yesterday. I don't even know her," he said with more than a hint of exasperation. "What's the point to all this?"

"I want you to be happy."

"I am happy," he said softly.

"I'm talking about when I'm gone." She met his gaze and held it. If he wanted her to stay this was the perfect time to tell her. All he had to do was say the word.

He gave her shoulder a squeeze then turned and grabbed the ladder. "Like I said, let's not even think about that now."

But it was all Claire could think about. That, and the fact that time was running out.

The Johnson-Kinisaw wedding was half-over, and Claire couldn't have said what had even happened. She sat in the back pew of the church immersed in her thoughts. Claire still didn't know where Tony stood. But she had decided that although Rachel liked Tony, he wasn't interested in her.

But that doesn't mean he won't be once you're gone.

The thought was surprisingly painful. Despite

what she'd said to Tony about hooking him up with Rachel, she couldn't bear to think of the two of them together.

Claire blinked back a few unwanted tears and took a deep breath. She'd known their arrangement was temporary. Hadn't they even joked about trying to make it last at least a month? But back then, she'd never planned on falling in love.

The realization was bittersweet. She'd never expected to love him. It had happened without her realizing it. Without her even wanting it to happen.

Tony's voice filled the church, and the band of hurt that had gripped her heart in a stranglehold tightened another notch. Hearing him talk about Christian love and commitment at a time when their relationship stood on the brink of dissolution was almost too much to bear.

Her eyes dropped to her hands, the sparkling ring trapping her gaze. How could she ever have thought it was ugly? She shifted her hand slightly, and the stone caught the overhead light.

How long would it be before he gave it to someone else? To a woman who would wear it proudly for a lifetime rather than just a month or two.

A lump filled her throat, and she forced her attention to the service. But watching the bride and groom light the unity candle only made matters worse.

Claire swallowed hard. Attending the wedding

had been a mistake. She should have insisted on staying downstairs and helping Mrs. Sandy, despite the woman's protests that everything was ready.

She and Mrs. Sandy had spent most of the afternoon getting the buffet set up and decorating the tables. There was nothing more to do but wait. The refrigerator was stocked with food ready to be set out, and Mrs. Sandy had the hot items warming in the ovens.

"Such a lovely couple," the older woman next to Claire said loudly. "They'll have beautiful children."

Claire looked up just in time to see the bride and groom head down the aisle. She breathed a sigh of relief and flashed the woman a smile. "They're both very attractive."

It was a simple statement, but it was all the encouragement the woman needed. To start spewing family history. She was the groom's great-aunt and she'd come all the way from Chicago for the wedding. Claire didn't even bother to feign an interested expression. She'd made the mistake of answering, and now she had to take her punishment and let the woman talk.

And talk she did. About how the two had been high school sweethearts. About how their love had survived four long years of separation at different colleges. About how their love was destined to last an eternity.

"They'll be together for the rest of the their lives." A dreamy smile crossed the lined face, and Claire knew the woman was a hopeless romantic.

It was the only reason she didn't bring up the story of her own parents who'd once vowed to love each other forever and didn't. Or use as an example one of her many friends who'd married right out of college and who were already divorced.

"Right now they think they'll love each other forever. But there's no guarantee that'll happen." The words on the tip of Claire's tongue popped out, surprising even her.

Behind her silver-rimmed glasses, the older woman's eyes widened.

A flash of heat shot up Claire's neck. "I'm sorry. It's a wedding. We shouldn't be talking divorce."

"My dear, don't apologize. I agree none of us knows what life holds in store. But I do believe if two people are committed to having a Christ-centered marriage, they don't have anything to fear."

Claire nodded, not wanting to say anything that might further the conversation. She glanced around and tried to see if there was a way that she could unobtrusively bypass being ushered out.

"My dear." The woman grasped her arm. It was as if she knew Claire was ready to bolt. "When you get a chance, look up Second Timothy one, verse seven. I think it'll help you understand what I'm talking about.''

Even though Claire doubted she'd have a chance to look up the verse, she thanked the woman and slipped out the side door.

Mrs. Sandy would be waiting, and for once Claire couldn't wait to get started. When you worked hard you didn't have time to think. Or worry.

Claire gazed in awe at her very own creation nestled inside the molded plastic container. She'd made the apple pie herself, with her own two hands. It smelled heavenly. And, while the lattice-like strips of crust may not be even, they were golden brown. It was truly a thing of beauty.

So were the biscuits, and remember how they tasted.

She shoved the thought aside and popped the lid over the top of the carrier. The biscuits had been a mistake. She'd rushed, and it had showed. But she'd taken her time with this pie, determined it would be perfect. It looked perfect. Now if it only tasted as good as it looked....

"I would have been glad to help you make the pie," Mrs. Sandy said for the tenth time.

"I know you would," Claire said. "But it was important to me that I do it myself."

Normally Claire would have gone out and

bought one, or at the very least been content with letting Mrs. Sandy make it. But this time it was different. This time Rachel would be there with her blond hair and blue eyes and award-winning peach pie.

And Claire refused to walk through Jocelyn's front door with a pie she hadn't made.

"Ready to go?" Tony stuck his head into the room, and Claire's heart picked up speed.

"As a matter of fact I am." Claire gave Mrs. Sandy a quick hug, then picked up the pie. "Thanks so much for talking me through this pie thing. I know it would have been faster to do it yourself."

Mrs. Sandy returned her hug. "We all have to learn sometime. If my mother hadn't taught me, I couldn't have taught you. Someday you'll teach your own daughter."

"Claire, we're running late," Tony warned.

"Coming, darling." She gave Mrs. Sandy a wink, feeling strangely happy and carefree. "Men. They're always in such a hurry."

"That's because—" he took the pie container from her arms and shot her a cocky smile "—women are always late."

They headed out the front door, and despite a light evening breeze the spicy scent of his after-shave surrounded her. She wrapped her arm through his. "You know I don't like to be teased."

"Really?" Tony chuckled. "I got the impression the other day that you liked it. A lot."

Her heart beat double time, remembering. "So, are you teasing me?"

"I hope so." Tony opened the car door and waited until she'd sat down before he handed her the pie. "Because I haven't been able to think of doing anything else all day."

Claire waited impatiently for Tony to round the front of the Jeep and slide behind the wheel. Then, before he could even put the key in the ignition, she leaned across the console, turned his face to hers with one hand and kissed him full on the lips.

This time she didn't rush, and neither did he. She put all the emotions that had been churning inside her into the kiss, and when they finally, reluctantly, separated, her insides trembled.

"Wow," Tony said. He raked his fingers through his hair. "That was worth waiting for."

"Tony." Claire ran her fingers lightly up his bare arm, and his muscles tensed beneath her touch. "You don't need to think of an excuse to kiss me. As far as I'm concerned, anytime is a good time."

Tony smiled, and that incredible dimple flashed in his cheek. "Anytime?"

Claire thought for a moment. Would there be a time when she wouldn't want Tony to kiss her?

No, she thought, but there *would* be a time when Tony wouldn't be around to kiss.

"That's right," she said. "Anytime works for me."

"I'm out." Tony laid his cards on the table and pushed back his chair.

His gaze scanned the room, looking for Claire. When they'd sat down to play cards, he'd been disappointed to find that all the couples had been separated. Adam had shrugged and told him it was Jocelyn's idea. It was her way of making sure everyone mingled.

Tony had definitely done his part. The way the game was structured, the winners got to stay together as partners while the losers had to split up and move. Since he'd lost far more games than he'd won, he'd had more than ample opportunity to interact with practically everyone.

Except Claire and her partner. They'd won every hand and hadn't moved once. His gaze lingered on her. He liked what she'd done with her hair, twisting it in a different kind of way. Claire was clearly the most attractive woman in the whole room. It was hard to believe she was with him.

He watched her slap down her last card with a flourish. She laughed in pure delight. Obviously it had been another winning hand. He smiled at her exuberance. Claire now found joy in the smallest things. Even things that in the past she wouldn't have given a second thought. Like this morning when she'd told him she'd learned how to make a bed with hospital corners. Or right before they left, when she'd showed him the pie she'd made all by herself.

Her masterpiece sat on a table against the far wall with five other pies. Unfortunately—and he'd never admit this to Claire—her apple looked like a plain Jane next to the pumpkin with streusel topping, the meringue with three-inch peaks or Rachel Taylor's sour cream peach.

"Looks like you're a loser, too." Almost as if she'd appeared when he'd thought her name, the slender blonde stood beside him.

"Loser?"

She gestured with her head toward the two couples still playing. "At cards."

"Yeah, well." Tony shrugged. "I've never been that much of a card player."

"Tim and Claire sure seem to have the magic touch."

He stared at her blankly.

"Tim," she prompted. "The guy I came here with."

"That's right. Your date." Tony remembered being introduced, but he hadn't talked to the guy since.

"Not my date," Rachel said firmly. "The guy I came with. There's a difference."

Tony smiled agreeably but didn't argue. Though he didn't see much difference, obviously she did.

"Claire and Tim certainly seem to get along well," Rachel said with an odd note in her voice.

Tony raised a brow.

"Since this is the first time they met and all," Rachel added quickly.

"Claire's very outgoing," Tony said.

"That'll be a real plus when she's a minister's wife." Rachel studied Tony carefully for a moment. "You two are getting married, right?"

He suddenly remembered Claire teasing him about Rachel, saying the woman had the hots for him. He'd brushed it off then. Now, seeing the look in Rachel's eyes, he suddenly wasn't so sure.

Tony shifted his gaze to Rachel. "That's the plan."

If he hadn't been looking for it, he might have missed the disappointment that skittered across the woman's features. Guilt sluiced through his veins. He'd never meant to give her the impression he was available. Or interested.

It was odd. When he'd been in the seminary and all his friends were getting married, he couldn't help but wonder what the woman would be like who he'd one day marry. Back then he'd pictured someone very much like Rachel. He knew she was a wonderful woman. The problem was there was already someone else in his heart.

"You two look so serious." Claire moved next to him, and he realized with a start the game must finally be over. "What's up?"

He draped his arm over her shoulder and smiled. "Actually Rachel and I were talking about you. Or rather about you and me. About our wedding."

Her dark eyes met his, and for a moment he lost himself in their depths.

"I love Claire's engagement ring," Rachel said, and Tony realized she was still standing there. "Didn't it once belong to a relative of yours?"

"It was my great-grandmother's engagement ring," Tony said.

"That is so romantic," Rachel said softly. "I can't imagine what it must be like to wear a family heirloom and know one day you'll hand it down to your son or daughter."

"If they want it," Tony said.

"Want it?" Rachel's voice was incredulous. "Of course they'd want it. Who wouldn't?"

Claire sighed and leaned back in the car seat, twisting the ring with her thumb. For one brief moment, she and Tony had connected. And in that instant she'd believed he'd wanted her as much as she wanted him.

Not in the physical way, although that pull was

definitely there, but in the forever-and-always sense. The until-death-do-us-part kind of thing.

But Rachel's words had severed that connection. And what could she have said? It wasn't the time to tell him she'd realized how wrong she'd been, with Rachel standing there hanging on every word.

And had she only imagined a distance, a coolness between them the rest of the evening? Only the fact that he'd taken a second piece of her pie, bypassing Rachel's sour cream peach entirely, had given her reason to hope.

The car pulled up in front of the bed-and-breakfast. Tony flicked off the lights.

Claire sat in the silence gathering her courage.

What if she'd read him wrong? What if he didn't return her feelings? She knew he was fond of her, liked kissing her, but did he love her?

"Claire." Tony spoke first, and in the darkness she couldn't see his eyes or read his expression. "Would you sit with me on the swing for a few minutes?"

She nodded and followed him up the steps. When he sat on the swing, she automatically took the spot next to him. His arm moved around her shoulders, and she leaned her head against his chest.

"Tony." Her fingers toyed with a button on his shirt, her voice muffled against his chest. "What's wrong?"

"Nothing. Everything." She could feel him sigh. "I'm not sure."

"I have a suggestion for you." The button slipped open.

Tony tensed and pushed her hand away. "Claire, kissing doesn't solve everything."

"What?" Claire closed the button with a single movement and lifted her head. She brushed her hair from her face with one hand. "You don't even know what I was about to say."

"I thought—"

"I know what you thought." Claire reached up and closed his mouth with her fingers. "But I was talking about praying."

"Really?" Tony shifted in his seat. "Since when did you become such a big fan of prayer?"

"Tony." Claire sat up straight. "I know this may come as a shock to you, but I do believe in God. And in the power of prayer."

"I didn't mean—"

"No," she said, interrupting him. "The words have been said. The harm is done."

He stared at her for a moment. Then his lips twitched. "How about you forgive me and we kiss and make up?"

"Tony, kissing doesn't solve anything."

"No, but it'll help clear my head." Tony smiled. "And, not to bring up promises, but you did say anytime."

She chuckled.

"And I'm a woman of my word." Claire lifted her face to his and pulled him to her. She was really going to miss this man.

Chapter Eleven

"**B**ut you *have* to know what kind of food you want at your reception." A thread of exasperation ran through Mrs. Sandy's voice. "The wedding is a week away."

Claire knew that better than Mrs. Sandy. Normally she would have been looking forward to the Fourth of July, the parades, the fireworks, even the picnics. But this year, Independence Day was also Judgment Day.

"Have you asked Tony?" Claire finished loading the dishwasher and straightened, wiping her hands on a tea towel.

Mrs. Sandy gave a frustrated cry. "Have I asked him?" She shut the kitchen cupboard door so hard the dishes rattled. "Only every day for the past two weeks."

Claire couldn't help but smile. And here she'd thought it was only her getting the pressure. Tony had never mentioned that Mrs. Sandy was harassing him, too.

"You two won't think it's so funny when you're feeding your guests peanut butter and jelly," Mrs. Sandy snapped.

Her words were sharp, but beneath the woman's gruffness Claire could sense the hurt, and she cursed her insensitivity.

"I'm sorry." Claire crossed the room and put her hand on Mrs. Sandy's arm. "You're right. Tony and I need to sit down and decide."

"I just want the day to be perfect," Mrs. Sandy said, smoothing a wrinkle in her apron. "I certainly don't mean to nag."

Claire stared at the woman who'd become so dear. She no longer saw the too-tight perm or the ample hips in the polyester pants. She saw a friend, someone who truly cared. And, she realized, that's what really mattered.

"This isn't your fault," Claire said firmly, meeting the woman's gaze. "You shouldn't have had to ask more than once. I'll talk to Tony and we'll get this settled."

"Thank you, Claire." Relief flooded Mrs. Sandy's face. "That's good news."

Unfortunately Claire knew it was anything *but* good news. Unless she took a big leap of faith and told Tony how she felt, she'd just signed her own walking papers.

"He wants to meet in Des Moines tonight?" Tony leaned back in his desk chair. "Why didn't he call me himself?"

Harold Clarke shrugged. "I know Larry tried to reach you. But he got your recorder and didn't want to leave a message. He and I are old friends so he called me thinking I might want to come, too."

Larry Babcock, Tony's pastoral advisor from the district office in Illinois, would be in Des Moines for the night. According to Harold, Larry and his wife wanted to take Tony out to dinner.

Although Larry seemed like a nice guy the one time they'd met, Tony knew he'd feel more comfortable if Harold joined them. "Are you going?"

"I'm afraid I can't." Harold shook his head, his voice filled with what sounded like genuine regret. "Darlene and I have tickets to some musical in Des Moines."

Tony hoped his surprise didn't show. He had no idea that Harold and Mrs. Sandy were seeing each other socially. But the more he thought about it, the more it made sense. Tony couldn't think of two people better matched. "Since you'll already be in Des Moines, why don't you stop by the restaurant before you go to the theater?"

"I thought of that," Harold said, "but Larry can't meet until seven and the musical starts at seven-thirty."

"That's too bad," Tony said.

"Will you be able to go?"

"I'll make it work." Tony mentally reviewed his schedule. "You say he's bringing his wife?"

"Yes," Harold said. "And they definitely want you to bring Claire."

Tony paused. "I'll be in Des Moines anyway for a prison ministry meeting. That runs from three to six-thirty. If I grab a ride with one of the other pastors, I could leave the Jeep for Claire. Then we can drive back together."

"Good plan." Harold smiled and handed Tony a piece of paper with the name and address of the restaurant in bold print. "Make sure you're on time. Larry's always been funny about being kept waiting."

"We'll be there." Tony glanced at the sheet. "Claire and I were planning to go out anyway, so there shouldn't be any conflicts."

"You've got yourself a nice woman, Tony," Harold said. "I don't mind telling you, at first I had a few doubts about how she'd like small-town living, but from what I've seen and what Darlene has told me, she's fitting in just fine."

Tony smiled. Not only had Claire become a part

of the town and the congregation, she'd become a part of his heart in the process.

"That wedding will be here before you know it," Harold said with a grin. "How many days is it?"

"Seven." Just saying the number brought the realization that time was running out.

If they held to their original agreement, he and Claire would break up soon. She'd return to Colorado, and he'd stay in Iowa. Alone.

But Tony was no longer sure that's what either of them wanted. During the past six weeks, Claire had become such a part of his life he couldn't imagine her not in it. And lately he'd started to believe she felt the same.

So why did he feel like a nervous schoolboy when he thought about telling her what was in his heart?

You know why.

Although he was ninety-nine percent sure she returned his feelings, a tiny voice deep within kept whispering the doubts. Claire was so beautiful, so wonderful. She could have her pick of any man. Why would she choose life with a small-town minister? Sure, she liked him, but did she love him? And, more importantly, did she love him enough to want to stay?

Tony squared his shoulders. There was only one way to know for sure. Tonight, he'd ask.

* * *

"Okay, we're set. We'll meet at the restaurant at seven," Tony said. "That means you'll have to leave here no later than six."

Claire could barely stop herself from coming back with some smart-mouth comment that would really get him going. She knew Tony wanted the evening to go perfectly, but this was getting ridiculous. She'd already sworn on a stack of Bibles she'd be on time.

"Tony, sweetheart, don't worry." She laid her hand against his cheek, and his skin was cool beneath her touch. "Haven't I already said I'd be there?"

"I know you have." Tony raked a hand through his hair. "But this is really important. This guy is the closest thing to a boss that I have."

"I realize that," Claire said, her last bit of patience gone. "That's why, unless something better comes up, I'll be there."

"Unless something better comes up?" He stared in disbelief.

"Just kidding," Claire laughed.

"Claire." He growled a warning.

"Tony." She shot him a saucy smile, but when his stony expression didn't soften, she gave in. "I'll be there."

"Will you?"

Claire tilted her head. Should she jerk his chain? Or be kind? ''Want me to write it in blood?''

Tony hesitated, and Claire thought for a minute he was going to take her up on the offer. Instead he smiled and reached up to brush a strand of hair from her face. ''Not necessary,'' he said. ''I...trust you.''

Claire exhaled. For a brief second she'd thought he was going to say he loved her. But once again, she'd been disappointed. She couldn't go on much longer like this, not knowing how he felt.

Claire squared her shoulders. There was only one way to know for sure. Tonight, after dinner when he wasn't so stressed, she'd ask.

Claire brushed her hair, smiling in satisfaction at the way the light from the bedroom window reflected off the dark shiny strands. She glanced at her nails, and her smile widened. After she'd left Tony this morning she'd splurged on a manicure at the local beauty shop.

The woman hadn't been as good as Yvette, who had done her nails for years, but the French manicure was more than adequate. The scent of the perfume Daddy had brought back from a midwinter trip to France lingered in the air. She'd taken a leisurely bath and then she'd applied it liberally to strategic pulse points, rubbing it in slowly, feeling the skin turn warm and fragrant beneath her touch.

This was it, D-day. Decision day. Tonight she'd lay her heart on the line and see what happened. Funny—she'd never before realized how scary it was to bare your soul to another.

All those times when men had professed to be in love with her, she'd never even considered what courage that simple act took. And remembering some of her responses—dear God, had she actually laughed once?—made her cringe.

If she hadn't had those experiences, it might be easier to take this step. Actually, she'd been hoping Tony would declare his feelings first. She could then say, "I love you, too," and they'd live happily ever after.

But he'd never said he loved her. He'd never asked if she'd consider staying forever. Oh, a few times he'd hinted that might be his preference. And the look in his eyes seemed to say he was a man in love, but he'd never said the actual words. Mrs. Sandy was right. Time was running out. They needed to talk.

If only she knew what would happen when they did. Claire glanced at her ring. Would it still be there tomorrow or would her finger be bare?

She lifted her gaze heavenward, desperate for some divine intervention.

Dear God, it's me, Claire. Tony says when we

pray we need to ask that Your will, not ours, be done. So, if it's Your will, please let Tony and me stay together. I think we could all benefit if I stayed in Millville. But if that's not in Your plan— Claire paused and swallowed hard—*please help me to accept it. Amen.*

The thought that God could have a different wife in mind for Tony stabbed Claire's heart like a knife. She didn't want to even think about that possibility. Not now.

The knock on the door was a welcome sound.

"Claire."

She recognized the voice immediately. Claire fastened her kimono tight around her waist. "Come in, April."

"I wanted to see if you had any red nail polish I could borrow." April's gaze lingered on Claire's silk robe and bare feet. Obviously she wasn't used to seeing anyone half dressed in the middle of the afternoon. Her eyes darted around the room. "Am I interrupting?"

"Not at all," Claire said, before she noticed the glint in April's eyes.

Oh, so that's what she was thinking.

Claire stifled a smile and kicked at the bed's dust ruffle. "Sorry to disappoint you, but I'm alone. No man stashed under the bed." She shifted her gaze pointedly across the room. "Or even in the closet."

April giggled. "I'm sorry. I don't know what I was thinking. You're too much of a Goody Two-shoes for that kind of thing."

"Really?" Claire raised a brow. Ever since she'd been old enough to date, she'd established a reputation as a party girl. And sometimes a tease. But never in her recollection had anyone ever called her a Goody Two-shoes.

And Claire wasn't sure she liked the picture it brought to mind. An image of her high school valedictorian, with her wire-rimmed glasses and a tissue clutched in one hand, flashed before her. "I've never thought of myself that way."

April shrugged and took a seat on the edge of the bed. "You can't help what you are."

Claire narrowed her gaze and reminded herself April was still young. And obviously stupid. She laid her brush down on the dressing table. "Whatever would make you think that about me?"

"Well…" April thought for a moment. "For one thing, you'd never think of sleeping with a guy before you were married."

"Actually I have," Claire said.

April inhaled sharply. Her eyes widened. She leaned forward in eager anticipation. "You and Pastor Karelli have—"

Claire laughed. "You've got it all wrong. I meant I'd *thought* about it. Not that I have *done* it."

"In youth group we learned that having the desire is the same as doing it."

"I know in God's eyes a sin is a sin," Claire said. "Personally I think there's a big difference between wanting to do something and actually doing it."

"So—" April picked a speck of nail polish off her thumb "—are you glad you've never done it?"

Claire paused and thought for a moment. This was an issue most teens faced, and Claire sensed April was no exception. The problem was Claire wasn't sure she should be the one to help. "Isn't this something you should discuss with your mother?"

"You want me to ask her if you're glad you've never had sex with our pastor?" April raised an innocent gaze. "How would she know?"

Claire laughed again. She wasn't sure April would have the nerve to approach her mother with such a question, but Claire could only imagine Mrs. Sandy's face if she did. "You're a crazy one, April Sandy."

"Yeah, I know. But you still haven't answered my question." The girl seemed unwilling to let the subject drop, and Claire knew she would have to give the girl some kind of answer.

She thought of all the times in the past she'd been tempted to cross that line, not just with Tony but with other guys she'd dated. Before Tony it hadn't been so much not doing it because of the right versus wrong thing, but more because of fear. Of letting anyone get too close.

But with Tony it was different. Somehow, without her even realizing it was happening, she'd let him and his God into her heart. And now, doing what was pleasing to God *did* matter.

"I *am* glad I've waited," Claire said finally. "The older I've gotten, the more I've realized that God knows what He's doing."

April studied her, her look clearly skeptical.

"You don't believe me," Claire said at last.

"Sure I do," April answered, a mischievous smile tipping her lips. "But I also think that you'll be happy to see the Fourth of July. I think you're ready to make some fireworks of your own."

"April!" Claire tried to feign a shocked look but couldn't quite pull it off. She ended up giggling.

"I only know that's how I'd be if I was marrying a hunk like Tony Karelli." April heaved an exaggerated sigh. "I just hope my blind date tonight turns out to be half as cute."

"Blind date?" Claire's surprise was genuine. No one had told her that April and what's-his-name had broken up. "What happened to..." She snapped her fingers, trying to recall the guy's name.

"Oh, him." April waved a dismissive hand. "He's long gone."

"What happened?"

"Too immature." April wrinkled her nose. "I like my men older."

Claire shook her head and wondered what April considered older. Nineteen? Twenty? She remembered the college guy she'd dated when she was seventeen. When you were that young a couple of years was a big difference.

"You better watch yourself, April." Even to her own ears, Claire sound more like a mother than the girl's peer. "Those older guys can be trouble."

"I can take care of myself," April said with the cocky insolence of youth. "Anyway, we're just going to the lake with some friends. Don't worry about me."

Claire hoped that was true. Right now she had her own problems to worry about. Time was flying, and she still needed to decide what she was going to wear. Tonight she wanted to look her best.

Two hours later Claire was convinced she'd succeeded. She'd chosen the red Versace. It fit as if it had been custom made for her figure, accentuating her curves without appearing too bold. The dress was one of her favorites.

She'd worn it a couple of weeks ago for the first time, and all night Tony couldn't keep his eyes off of it. Or her. Anticipation surged, and Claire glanced at the clock, eager for the evening to begin.

She could leave early, but what would be the point? Tony would be lucky to get to the restaurant five minutes early. Plus, Claire found she rather enjoyed having the house to herself.

Being alone gave her time to think. And plan.

What would he say when she told him she loved him? Would he be surprised? Shocked?

The ringing phone intruded on her thoughts, and Claire waited for April to grab it. Until she realized April had long ago left for the lake. Claire picked up the receiver.

"Hello."

"It's April."

April spoke so softly Claire had to strain to hear her. She wondered if the girl was on her cell phone. "April, could you speak up?"

"I can't." Despite the bad connection, Claire could hear the tremble in April's voice. "Claire, you've got to come and get me. I'm at the Nordstrom place, north of town."

Claire remembered the farm. There had been a barn fire there several weeks before, and she and Tony had gone out to see if there was anything they could do to help. "What are you doing there? I thought you were at the lake."

"I can't talk. Just come. Please."

The phone went dead. Claire paused, the receiver still cradled in her hand. A shiver traveled up her spine. Something was very wrong. The Nordstroms were in Illinois visiting their daughter. And their youngest son, Wayne, had to be at least twenty-two or twenty-three. He was way too old to be in April's crowd.

I'm going on a blind date. With an older guy.

Surely April wasn't there with Wayne Nordstrom. But even as she hoped that wasn't the case, a sick feeling in the pit of her stomach told her that was a very real possibility.

She'd met Wayne the day of the fire, and she hadn't liked him. Not only did he have that youthful arrogance she found so unappealing, he'd looked her up and down as if she was one of his dad's prime head of beef and he hadn't eaten in a while.

Trying not to panic, Claire quickly reviewed her options. Mrs. Sandy and Tony were both out of town. Even if she could reach them, it would take over an hour for them to get back.

Claire grabbed her purse just as the clock chimed six in the background. She was going to be late for dinner, but it couldn't be helped. The unfortunate thing was she couldn't even call Tony and tell him what was happening. His meeting wouldn't be over until six-thirty, and his cell phone would be turned off until then.

Tony would be disappointed she wasn't there on

time. But he'd never want her to let a friend down. April needed her help, and Claire couldn't desert her.

She pulled her keys from her purse and headed out the door. Claire started the Jeep and headed down the road. She said a little prayer. That April would be okay. That she would be able to help. And that Tony would understand.

Chapter Twelve

The Nordstrom house sat a quarter mile back from the road. Two rows of cedar trees lined each side of a gravel drive leading to the two-story house.

Claire pulled into the farmyard, recognizing Wayne's tan pickup immediately. But she'd never seen the Mercedes convertible next to it. Between the hundred-year-old house with its peeling paint and the rusty pickup that was probably new when Reagan was in the White House, the car was as out of place as Claire.

Claire wheeled Tony's Jeep into the space between the car and the truck. She hoped April was overreacting. Claire took the front steps two at a time and prayed that was the case.

The door opened immediately, and Claire stared.

Before her was probably the most gorgeous man she'd ever seen in person. Eyes as blue as the shiny finish on the Mercedes glittered at her.

Claire knew she'd never met this guy before, but she recognized him at once. There was no way any woman could forget that face. He was classically handsome with finely shaped features and hair the color of spun gold. The man's lips widened in a broad smile. His teeth were straight and white, as perfect as the rest of him.

"Welcome." He opened the door wide and motioned her in. "April said she'd called a friend. She just didn't tell us you were so pretty."

It was the type of comment that Claire normally took in stride...even expected. But with April's call fresh in her mind, a deep sense of unease settled over her.

"I don't believe we've met." She stuck out her hand. "I'm Claire Waters."

"Jay Nordstom." He took her hand, and his palm was soft and smooth.

"I've heard all about you." She finally remembered where she'd seen him. "You're Millville's big success story. The town's golden boy who's on the cover of this month's *GQ*. I thought your mother said you lived in LA."

"I do." Jay chuckled, even though Claire couldn't see what was funny. "Ever been there?"

It was all she could do not to laugh out loud.

She wanted to tell him she'd probably been in more major cities than he'd ever dreamed of seeing, but instead she just smiled. "No, but I've been to Des Moines…once."

He chuckled again and draped his arm around her shoulders, ushering her inside. "Next month *People* magazine is doing a feature on me."

"Wow." Claire widened her eyes and tried to keep the sarcasm from her voice. "I wished I'd brought my autograph book."

He stared for a moment as if trying to figure out if she was really impressed. Little did he know she'd grown up around famous people, beautiful people her whole life. Though she found it easier to look at a pretty face than an ugly one, Jay's smug arrogance was a turnoff.

Claire and Tony had both heard all about him and his skyrocketing career the day of the fire. While his father had been busy with the insurance adjuster, his mother had entertained Claire and Tony with pictures of Jay and tales of his life in the big city.

Tony had been less than attentive that morning, and Claire had been in the mood to stir things up. She'd deliberately played to Mrs. Nordstrom's pride in her son, telling her she agreed he *was* the handsomest man she'd ever seen and how wonderful to be so successful at twenty-eight. Tony didn't seem to pay any attention until she said something about Jay being every woman's dream man. When his eyes narrowed and he glared at her, Claire knew she'd made her point.

"I think you and I are going to have fun." Jay's gaze slid seductively up and down Claire's figure.

He and his brother were obviously two of a kind.

"Are you ready to party?"

"Maybe." Claire shrugged. "Let me talk to April and see what she has planned."

Jay snorted. "All she wants to do is go home."

"Not into partying, huh?" Claire kept her tone deliberately light and offhand.

Jay moved closer, and the overpowering smell of alcohol hit her. It was all she could do not to step back. Even though Jay wasn't staggering or slurring his words, he'd obviously downed more than a couple of drinks this afternoon. "Not like I am."

Claire paused. "I guess I could take her home and come back later."

"Neither of you are going anywhere," Jay said, and a shiver shot up her spine. "We're playing this my way. Got that?"

Claire stared at him. She'd dealt with men like him before. Guys who thought that every woman secretly wanted them. Guys who wouldn't take no for an answer.

She smiled and linked her arm with his. "Why

don't you be hospitable and get me something to drink?''

"Now that's more like it." Jay's smile widened. "We've got Bud. Or Jack."

Claire stifled a groan.

"I'll take a Bud." She could barely force the word past her lips. "Where's April? Maybe she wants one, too."

"She's busy with Wayne." Jay jerked his head toward a closed door. "You'd better knock before you enter. Wayne might be finally getting some."

Claire's heart rose to her throat. If something happened to April, she'd never forgive herself. She rapped her knuckles against the door and pushed it open at the same time.

"How many times do I have to tell ya. I'm not taking you home." Wayne's words were loud and slurred. He stood towering over April. In that instant Claire decided that being ugly and drunk was a horrible combination.

"You can't keep me here." April sat perched on the edge of an overstuffed chair, her arms folded tightly across her chest. Her chin jutted out in a defiant tilt, and her eyes appeared too large for her face.

"April?"

"Claire." A look of joy flashed across the girl's pale face. She jumped up, flew across the room and wrapped her arms tightly around Claire. "I knew you'd come."

Wayne popped a handful of sunflower seeds in his mouth and narrowed his gaze. "About time you got here."

Claire forced a laugh and pried April's arms from her. "I came right over. There's nothing I like more than a good party."

Confusion clouded April's gaze. "But I want to go home."

"I told you." Wayne took a big swig from a long-necked bottle, then belched loudly. "You're not going anywhere."

"I want to leave." April spoke in the same low, shaky voice she'd used on the phone. "But he won't let me."

Claire's smile never wavered. April was scared, but there wasn't much Claire could do about it now.

"Here you go." Jay entered the room with three bottles hanging loosely from one hand. He handed one to Claire, another to his brother and held out the last to April.

The girl shook her head and pressed her lips together, as if she was afraid he'd pour it down her throat.

"Suit yourself." Jay flipped off the top and took a long drink. His gaze shifted from April to Claire before moving to Wayne. "Looks like this may work out after all, bro. One for you and one for me.''

"I brought April for you," Wayne said loudly. He turned and pointed to Claire. "I want that one."

"Get real." Jay's blue eyes turned to a steely gray. "I don't want any kid."

"I'm not doing anything with either of you." April's eyes flashed. "And you can't make me."

Both men stood well over six feet, and it was obvious they worked out regularly. April was dead wrong on this one. If they chose to force the issue, neither she nor Claire would stand a chance.

What Claire needed was to buy them some time. Her gaze shifted to the deck of cards on the coffee table. Jocelyn had said everyone in Iowa loved cards. She hoped her friend was right. "I want to play—"

"I'm not going to play any stupid card game," Wayne said, interrupting her.

"Wayne," Claire said in a teasing tone, "didn't your mother teach you to let a lady finish talking?" She softened her words with a smile. "Now I bet you like poker."

"Strip poker." Jay leered.

"How about you, Wayne?"

Wayne's gaze shifted to April. "Sounds good to me."

April gasped.

The plan wasn't quite evolving as Claire had planned. Still, she might be able to salvage it.

"I might be up for it." Claire shrugged. "But you're going to have to send the kid home." She jerked her thumb in April's direction. "She's jailbait. And neither of you needs that kind of hassle."

"But," Wayne blustered, "if we let her leave, we'll be one short."

"If you play your cards right," Claire said with a sly smile, "you can both be winners."

April's hands shook so badly she could barely keep the Jeep on the road. She'd been shocked when the guys had said she could go.

She wasn't sure if it had more to do with the jailbait comment or Claire's offer. She suspected the latter.

Their eyes had lit up, and they'd been practically drooling when Claire had laid out the terms. She would play against the two of them. If the men won, she'd take them both on. If she won, she'd get to pick which brother she wanted.

April knew they'd say yes. Claire had never looked more beautiful, and the looks the two shot each other told her they knew the odds were in their favor.

They'd practically shoved April out the door. Claire had barely had time to whisper the plan.

April stepped on the gas. Although the guys had

several layers of clothing they could take off, Claire didn't. And with that type of temptation who knew what the brothers would do, regardless of anything Claire would say. It wouldn't take long before...

Shoving the disturbing thought aside, April forced her attention to the road. She wheeled the Jeep into the parking lot of the gas station at the edge of town and headed inside to the pay phone.

She had to dial the number of the sheriff's office twice before she got it right.

"Dispatch. State your emergency."

The moment April heard the official-sounding voice, she decided she couldn't tell them everything. She'd be in big trouble if they knew it all.

"I was driving by the Henry Nordstrom place on Bluff Road. They're out of town and there was a strange car there. It looked like someone was trying to break in. Please hurry."

"We'll send someone right out." The impersonal female voice could have been a recording. "May I get your name?"

April slammed the receiver down, her heart beating so rapidly she thought for a moment she might faint. Claire had only said to call the sheriff. The rest April had come up with on her own.

She prayed the sheriff would go out even though she hadn't left her name. But even more than that, she prayed Claire knew how to play poker.

* * * *

"Are you sure you gave her the right address?" Larry Babcock glanced at his watch, and Tony resisted the urge to sneak a peek at his, as well.

Only the thought that he'd checked it less than five minutes before stopped him.

Claire was over an hour late. They'd finally given in and ordered. Larry's stomach had growled so loudly it was a wonder the waitress could hear the order.

Tony took a bite of his salad and pretended not to notice the glances between Larry and his wife. This looked bad, not only for him, but for Claire, as well.

If she was just running late, why hadn't she called?

I'll be there...unless something better comes along.

Her words had been teasing, not serious. She knew how important this evening was to him.

He swallowed the lettuce that tasted like paper and washed it down with a gulp of iced tea. There had to be a good reason she hadn't showed. There simply had to be.

"Read 'em and weep." Claire laid down her hand and smiled broadly. "Four aces."

Wayne cursed and flung his cards on the table.

He jerked his T-shirt over his head and tossed it across the room in disgust.

Jay laughed and reached for the zipper of his shorts. ''For the first time I can say I'm glad I haven't given up underwear.''

The game had gone just as she'd planned. Poker was her father's favorite game, and not only had he taught Claire all she knew about the game, he'd taught her a few tricks, as well. Tricks that under normal circumstances could be considered cheating. Today they were necessary tools for self-preservation. And they'd worked.

Since the game began she'd only lost two hands, and those she'd deliberately thrown. Her pair of shoes went first, the panty hose next. Jay had retrieved the nylons from the floor and draped them around his neck like a lei.

But Claire knew if the sheriff didn't get here soon, she'd be forced to throw another hand, just to make it look good. The trouble was, she didn't know what else she could afford to lose.

She took another sip of her beer, just for show. The bottle was still over half full.

''Deal the cards, Wayne.'' She held up the bottle and spoke loudly, getting into the role she'd been forced to play. ''I feel lucky.''

''What in the name of—''

Claire turned toward the doorway, the man's

words partially muffled by the rock music blaring from the stereo.

Jay shoved back his chair and rose. He walked nonchalantly to the entertainment unit and hit the power button. "There, that's better."

He turned and glanced at the sheriff. "To what do we owe this honor?"

The officer's gaze took it all in, Jay standing there as confidently as if he was in a suit and tie instead of clad only in his Jockey shorts with Claire's panty hose around his neck, Wayne, naked from the waist up, sitting at the table, and Claire in her silk dress and pearls, holding a bottle of beer between her fingers.

Claire could only imagine the picture they made.

"We got a report of a break-in. I knocked but no one answered. The door was open, so I just thought I'd check things out."

Thank you, God.

"Well, Sheriff, nothing is going on here, 'cept a friendly little game of strip poker." Jay smiled. "That's not against the law, is it?"

The sheriff's gaze lingered on Claire, and she could tell he remembered her from church. He didn't even try to hide his disapproval. "No, there's no *law* against it."

"There you have it." Wayne belched and shuffled the cards. "Now if you'll excuse us..."

"Gladly." The sheriff turned to go, and Claire shoved back her chair.

"Sheriff, I was wondering if you might give me a ride back to town?"

He stared at her for a long moment. "Sure."

"Thanks." She walked over and grabbed her nylons from Jay's neck and her shoes from the table in front of Wayne. "See you later, guys."

"You're not leaving." Confusion warred with anger in Jay's azure eyes. "We were just getting started."

"That's where you're wrong," Claire said, lighthearted with relief. She stuffed her nylons into her purse and slipped on her shoes. "This game's over."

All the way to the cruiser, the officer kept his gaze fixed straight ahead. It wasn't until they were settled in that he spoke. "I know this is none of my business, but what was going on back there?"

Claire ignored the question. She knew it looked bad, but there had been drinking going on, and April was underage. Anything she said would implicate April. "Mind telling me how you happened to stop by?"

"Dispatch got an anonymous report of a possible break-in." The deputy's mirrored sunglasses hit his eyes "You wouldn't know anything about that, would you?"

"Me?" Claire laughed. "Why would I call?"

"You tell me." The deputy tilted his head questioningly. "Dispatch said it was a woman that called. You seemed awfully eager to get out of there."

"I was getting bored." Claire lifted a shoulder in a careless shrug.

"How long have you known Jay Nordstrom?"

"Is this an interrogation?" Claire raised a brow. "Am I under arrest?"

"What would I charge you with? You're over twenty-one," he said. "You can booze it up with a hundred guys if you want. Although I'm not sure Pastor Karelli would approve."

"I guess that's between him and me, isn't it?" Claire narrowed her gaze. She didn't appreciate his tone and she certainly didn't deserve his censure, but the less she said the better.

"I guess it is," he said, his lips pressed in a tight disapproving line. "I'd still like to know what happened."

Claire stared out the window as if fascinated by the rolling farmland.

The ten miles into town seemed like an eternity. Claire could feel the deputy's watchful eyes studying her but she pretended not to notice. She glanced at her watch. Seven-thirty. Too late to leave for Des Moines.

An image of Tony's worried face flashed before

her. He'd been so concerned she might let him down. And now she had.

No, you didn't. You saved a friend. Exactly what he would have done.

She had no idea what might have happened, but she couldn't take that chance. Tony would understand about missing dinner, although he might scold her for putting herself at risk. But then she and Tony would probably have a good laugh about it. After all, she'd beaten the pants off Jay and Wayne. It was really pretty funny when you thought about it.

Wasn't it?

Chapter Thirteen

April sat on the step of the front porch and watched Claire get out of the sheriff's car. She had to stop herself from racing across the yard to make sure Claire was okay. But since she wasn't sure what Claire had told the deputy, she decided to play it cool.

At least Deputy Crouse had got the call. He'd only been in Millville for a couple of years, and the word around town was he took his job seriously. April hoped that meant he'd keep his mouth shut.

She narrowed her gaze. Claire looked fine, but then April had learned looks could be deceiving. Take Wayne and Jay, for example.

A rush of unease coursed through April. She'd started to worry ever since she'd called the sheriff.

Had she overreacted? The more she thought, the more she realized that neither guy had actually threatened her.

"You want to go inside?" Claire said.

For the past hour April had done nothing but think of what she was going to say to Claire, what questions she would ask her. Now that the time had arrived, her tongue seemed tied in knots and a nervous burning filled the pit of her stomach. "Sure. I can make us some lemonade if you want."

Claire wrinkled her nose. "I don't think beer and lemonade really make such a good combination."

"You drank with them?" April said, unable to hide her surprise.

"I *am* over twenty-one," Claire laughed.

A surge of relief hit April. Obviously whatever had happened couldn't have been *too* traumatic if Claire could still laugh.

"Actually I only drank half a bottle," Claire continued, "just enough to convince them I was one of the boys. Unfortunately it was more than enough to leave a bad taste in my mouth."

"I could get you a glass of ice water," April said eagerly. "Or maybe you'd like some tea better?"

Claire's expression softened, and she stopped to

give the girl's shoulder a squeeze. "You didn't do anything wrong, April. You were right to call me."

April didn't answer. She couldn't. She followed Claire inside and let the front screen door fall shut with a bang. "I'm not so sure."

"April." Claire stopped suddenly and spun around, her dark eyes flashing. "You didn't know what they were going to do. They were older. They were much bigger. And there were two of them."

"But—"

"No buts. You did the right thing." Claire's tone broached no argument. "The only thing I can't figure out is what you were doing there in the first place."

She said it as a statement, not a question, but April knew Claire expected an answer. The soft hum of the dishwasher filled the silence. April glanced around the spotless kitchen, stalling for time. "Looks like somebody got dinner all cleaned up."

"April." Claire shot her a warning glance.

"Okay." April sighed and gestured to a chair at the table and took the seat opposite Claire. "I went to the lake, and my blind date never showed. Then everyone split into couples, and I was the oddball. Even Matt had someone."

April heaved a disgusted sigh. Seeing Matt with that sleazy Dana had been the last straw.

"Matt?" Claire raised a brow.

"Coukle. My old boyfriend."

Confusion still shown on Claire's face, and April couldn't believe she didn't remember Matt. He was one of the coolest guys in town. "You met him the first night you were here. You called him Matt Cuckoo."

Claire's lips curved upward. "Now I remember."

"Anyway," April said, wishing she could just forget it all but knowing Claire deserved an explanation, "I didn't want to look like this big loser, so when Wayne stopped by he and I sorta hooked up. Then he mentioned his brother, Mr. Famous Model, was in town and asked if I wanted to meet him. I said sure, but I swear I didn't know his parents were out of town."

April knew she sounded defensive, but she couldn't help it. Her mother would kill her if she found out she'd been alone with the Nordstrom boys.

"What happened then?" Claire said.

"It wasn't until I got in Wayne's truck and we were halfway to his house that I realized he'd been drinking."

Claire's look was clearly skeptical. April understood. It was hard for her to believe she'd been so stupid. But she'd been anxious to get away from Matt.

"After we got there it only got worse. Wayne

was chugging one beer after another. Jay was drinking beer *and* doing shots." April pressed her eyes shut to stop the tears welling up. She took a deep breath. "I got scared and told them I wanted to go home, but they got mad. That's when I called you."

She met Claire's gaze. "I am so sorry I dragged you into this."

Claire opened her mouth but April didn't give her the chance. "I mean, you were all dressed up to go out...."

The realization hit her like a ton of bricks. She'd thought she couldn't feel any worse. Now she knew she'd been wrong about that, too. "You had that fancy dinner in Des Moines tonight."

"It wasn't that fancy." Claire's smile didn't quite reach her eyes. "It couldn't be. It was in Des Moines, after all."

Claire emphasized the silent S, and April had to smile. But then she remembered how pumped Claire had been for this dinner, and her smile disappeared. "Tony was expecting you."

"Yes, he was." The last of the light faded from Claire's eyes. "But I'm sure he'll understand."

"You're going to tell him what happened?" April's heart sank. She'd thought...she'd hoped this would stay between the two of them.

"I have to," Claire said. "I don't want there to be any secrets between Tony and me."

"But you won't tell anyone else, will you?" April drew a deep shuddering breath. Her skin felt hot and clammy at the same time. "Promise me, Claire. Promise me you won't tell anyone else."

Claire finished the glass of tea April had forced on her and headed up the stairs, wishing Tony were home so she could explain and have this over with.

She undressed, carefully hanging her dress on the padded hanger so it wouldn't wrinkle. She put her necklace and earrings in the jewelry case.

Too restless to nap or read, Claire decided to go for a walk. Normally she wasn't much for physical exertion, but she'd gone running a couple of times with Tony and despite her reluctance had ended up enjoying herself. She pulled on a pair of black running shorts and a T-shirt. Not until she had laced her shoes, clasped her hair back with a barrette and headed out the front door did Claire allow herself to think about all that had happened this evening.

Would Tony understand that she'd done what she did with the best of intentions? Or would he think her incredibly stupid? Or, worse yet, believe it was just a ploy to get out of the dinner?

She shoved the thought aside and picked up the pace. Her feet slapped against the asphalt surface of the trail, the rhythmic beat of her footfalls oddly reassuring. Funny—she'd never liked to exercise before she got involved with Tony.

By the time she reached the downtown district and turned back, her breath came in short, fast puffs. But the tension that had gripped her neck in a stranglehold had eased, and once again she felt at peace.

She lifted her gaze to the darkening sky. *Dear God, I know I shouldn't worry, that I should just turn my fears over to You. So I'm ready now to give them away. If You want them, please take them. Amen.*

If her gaze had been focused earthward, Claire might have seen the tiny dog dart across the path. And if she had seen it, she might not have fallen.

Where was she?

Tony glanced at his watch in annoyance. He'd been home for half an hour, and there'd been no sign of Claire. Or of anyone else, for that matter.

It looked as if April had gone to bed early, and Mrs. Sandy must still be out with Harold. But where was Claire? And why hadn't she shown up tonight?

Unless I get a better offer...

The words kept running through his head, even though he kept reminding himself she'd only been kidding.

A car engine sounded in the driveway. Tony jumped up and hurried to the door.

He jerked it open. "About time you..."

The words died in his throat. It wasn't Claire who stood in the porch light's soft glow, but Mrs. Sandy and Harold Clarke.

Harold cleared his throat and took a step back. Only then did Tony realize he'd interrupted a good-night kiss.

"I'm sorry." Tony raked his fingers through his hair. Would nothing go right this evening? "I thought you were Claire."

"Claire?" Mrs. Sandy's brow furrowed. "Isn't she with you?"

"She was supposed to be...."

They followed Tony into the living room, and he quickly filled them in on what had transpired.

"So when I got home and the Jeep was parked out front, I assumed she was here." His gaze shifted between the two, and he could see his own fears reflected on their faces.

"Maybe you should call the sheriff," Harold said.

"And say what?" As tempting as the idea was, Tony wasn't sure the sheriff would take a missing persons report on someone gone less than six hours. "That she stood me up for dinner and wasn't here when I got home?"

Mrs. Sandy gently touched his arm. "But she promised to meet you."

"I know." Tony didn't know whether to be

worried or angry. For the moment he was a little of both. "She said I could count on her."

Unless something better came along.

Once again he shoved the thought aside. How could he seriously consider that? After all this time he knew what she was like, didn't he?

"Tony."

His head jerked up and he flushed. "I'm sorry. I didn't hear you. I was thinking about Claire."

Harold's expression softened. "I really think you need to give the sheriff a call."

Tony opened his mouth to protest, but Harold raised a hand. "I know you don't want to bother them, but this isn't D.C. Around here we look after our own."

"Mrs. Perkins down the street even calls them when her cat runs off," Mrs. Sandy added.

Tony had to smile. Mrs. Perkins's cat weighed over twenty-five pounds, and Tony doubted it could run anywhere. Still, what they were saying made sense. After all, what did it hurt to call? The worst that could happen was they'd ask him to check back tomorrow.

"Okay. I'll give it a shot."

Mrs. Sandy nodded approvingly and glanced pointedly at Harold. "We'll go into the kitchen and make some coffee. The number's in the front of the phone book."

Tony flipped open the book, found the listing

immediately and dialed the number. He quickly explained the situation to the dispatcher. To his surprise, she didn't put him off, but promised to send someone right over.

He hung up the phone and rested his head in his hands. If anything happened to Claire, he didn't know what he'd do.

Dear God, please keep her safe.

"Tony?" Mrs. Sandy lightly touched his shoulder. "What did they say?"

Tony blinked rapidly before glancing up. "They're sending a deputy right over."

As if on cue the doorbell rang.

"I'll get it." Mrs. Sandy bustled out of the room.

Tony pushed back his chair and Harold came out of the kitchen, a cup of coffee in each hand. He shoved one of the mugs at Tony.

"I'm not—"

"Drink it," Harold said in a no-nonsense tone. "We may have a long night ahead of us."

Tony took the cup and took a sip. The extra-strong brew burned his throat. He almost relished the pain.

Footsteps sounded in the hall, and Mrs. Sandy escorted a uniformed officer into the room. Tony recognized him from his men's Bible study class.

"Tony, I believe you know Deputy Crouse."

Tony stepped forward and extended his hand. "Mark, thank you for coming."

"That's what we're here for, Pastor." The man took Tony's hand in a firm grip. "I was in the neighborhood when dispatch called, so I came right over."

"Harold, why don't we go into the kitchen and leave these two to talk their business?" Mrs. Sandy turned to the deputy. "Mark, can I get you a cup of coffee? Maybe a piece of cheesecake?"

Despite the seriousness of the situation, Tony had to smile. Trust Mrs. Sandy to be the perfect hostess.

"No, thanks." The deputy took off his hat and sat down.

"Darlene," Tony said, "I'd like it if you and Harold would stay."

Her face softened. "Of course."

Tony leaned back in his chair and gazed at the deputy. A look almost like sympathy flickered in the man's eyes. A tightness gripped Tony's chest.

"Mark, do you know what's happened to Claire?"

"I'm not sure where she is now, Pastor."

Tony's heart sank. "What do you mean now?"

"Well, I knew where she was earlier this evening."

Tony leaned forward, a mixture of dread and

anticipation coursing through his veins. ''Where was she?''

Officer Crouse looked up and met his gaze. ''In my patrol car.''

Chapter Fourteen

If his heart hadn't been beating so loudly Tony would have sworn it had stopped. It was hard enough to breathe, much less talk, but he had to know Claire was okay.

"Was she...?" His voice broke. He steadied himself and tried again. "Was she hurt?"

Deputy Crouse shook his head. "She's fine."

"Thank God." Mrs. Sandy's voice trembled, and Harold put his arm around her shoulders.

Tony exhaled a relieved breath and sent his own prayer of thanks heavenward.

"But if she wasn't hurt, then why was she in your patrol car?" Harold voiced Tony's question.

"And where is she now?" Mrs. Sandy added.

The deputy's gaze shifted from Tony to Mrs. Sandy to Harold to Tony. He hesitated.

"Mark." Tony leaned forward and rested his elbows on his knees. "I'm worried about her. Please tell me what's going on."

He cast a sideways glance at Harold and Mrs. Sandy. "I think it would be best if we spoke privately."

"Of course," Harold said, looking at Mrs. Sandy. "Darlene and I—"

Tony raised a hand and cut the church elder off mid-sentence. "You and Darlene are like family to me. I want you to stay."

"Pastor, I don't think..." The deputy shoved his hands into his pockets and rocked on his heels.

"Mark, it's okay. Just tell us what happened." Tony took a deep breath and steeled himself. It had to be serious to keep Claire from meeting him. "And don't leave anything out."

"Well." Mark glanced at the clock. He cleared his throat. "A call came into dispatch late this afternoon reporting a possible intruder at the Nordstrom place."

Tony kept his gaze fixed on the deputy.

"Anyway—" Mark ran his finger around the inside of his collar as if it had suddenly grown too tight "—there was a car I didn't recognize out front, and the door was half open, so I went in."

"But what does this have to do with Claire?" Mrs. Sandy said, her look clearly puzzled.

"I'm getting to that."

"Darlene, let the deputy talk," Harold said.

"You were saying?" Tony didn't bother to hide his impatience. Would Mark ever get to the point?

"The minute I stepped into the dining room, I saw them. The two guys and Ms. Waters." Mark's mouth tightened.

"Had she been kidnapped?" With a hiss of alarm, Tony leaned forward. Dear God, he'd been sitting in a restaurant eating while she'd been in danger.

"Not hardly." There was a moment of strained silence until the deputy spoke again. "I knew right away there'd been no break-in. I recognized Wayne and Ms. Waters immediately. Jay took me a while longer."

Part of Tony's brain whispered a warning that maybe he should content himself with the knowledge that Claire was okay and not go poking into things he was better off not knowing. But he couldn't stop himself. "What were they doing?"

"From the looks of it…having their own little party."

"You'd better explain that statement, son," Harold said, his expression grim. "In case you've forgotten, this is Tony's intended that you're talking about."

"I know it is, sir." The deputy's eyes flashed, and Tony could see that man had taken Harold's comment as a personal attack. "But tell me what you'd call it when you walk into a room littered with beer bottles and the three of them are sitting at the table playing strip poker? Wayne was half naked—didn't have his shirt—and the only thing keeping Jay from being in his birthday suit were his Jockey shorts.''

"But how do you know Claire was involved?" Harold said.

The deputy shifted his gaze to the man. "Because she had cards in one hand, a beer bottle in the other and her nylons were draped around Jay's neck."

"I don't believe it." Mrs. Sandy clasped a hand to her throat. "Claire would never be a part of something like that. And I've never seen her drink beer."

"She was drinking today," the deputy said, throwing Tony a look of apology. "I smelled it on her."

"I still don't believe it," Mrs. Sandy said, her chin set in a stubborn tilt. "There has to be a logical explanation. Claire would never—"

Tony waved her silent, trying to comprehend what he'd just heard.

"The one guy was in his underwear?" His voice sounded faraway even to his own ears. Why he continued to grill the deputy for details, Tony wasn't sure. Maybe because he still couldn't believe Claire would be a part of anything like this.

"Yes, sir." The deputy's lips quirked upward, and Tony wanted to throttle him. "And it didn't seem to bother him. Jay Nordstrom may have grown up around here, but he's a California boy now. That's a whole different world."

"Excuse me," Tony interrupted and tried to put the pieces of the confusing puzzle together in his suddenly numb brain. "Are you saying the guy in his underwear was a Nordstrom?"

"Jay's the oldest son," Mrs. Sandy said. "He's the one that's the big-time model in L.A."

Now he remembered. Every woman's dream man.

Tony tried to still the pain welling up in him.

"I thought I mentioned that," Mark said. "It was just the three of them, the two Nordstrom boys and your fiancée."

My fiancée.

A picture of Claire playing strip poker with her dream man while he'd sat for hours in that restaurant waiting and worrying flashed before him.

What could have made her do it? Had she decided their relationship would be over soon and it was time to move on to greener pastures? Maybe it was best after all that he hadn't confessed his feelings and asked her to marry him.

How could he have been so wrong? It was bad enough she'd discredited herself in Harold's eyes, but he'd never thought she'd do anything to hurt him. Obviously he'd been wrong to believe she'd changed. And he'd been foolish to think she loved him. He was lucky to find out the truth.

Tony swallowed hard past the lump in his throat.

The trouble was, he didn't feel lucky. Not at all.

Claire stopped short. The house was ablaze with lights. In the driveway, next to Tony's Jeep, sat a silver Cadillac she vaguely remembered. Down the street a black and white cruiser turned the corner and disappeared.

Ripples of panic turned her skin to gooseflesh. Why would Officer Crouse stop at the house? She hadn't broken any laws, so he couldn't have come about that. Maybe he hadn't come for her. Maybe he'd found out that April had been at the Nordstrom farm.

Claire drew a deep, shuddering breath. April had so much going for her. The girl didn't need this kind of trouble. Going with Wayne had just been a foolish mistake. She certainly didn't deserve to pay for it with a juvenile record. And, if Claire had anything to say about it, she wouldn't.

She straightened her shoulders and, forgetting everything but her desire to save the girl, headed up the stairs. She jolted to a stop. Pain shot up her leg, and her breath caught in her throat. She didn't dare look down. Her ankle had started to swell the minute she'd picked herself up after tripping over that dog, and she didn't even want to know what it looked like now.

It had taken her three times as long as it should to make her way home, and if she hadn't found a stick to use as a crutch she'd still be walking.

Now if she could just make it up three more steps. She took a deep breath, clenched her teeth and concentrated on the stairs. First one foot and then the other, until finally she reached the porch. Another few feet and she stood at the door.

It was slightly ajar, and through the screen she could hear Tony's rich baritone mingling with other voices.

Her heart sank. She'd hoped to catch him alone. Telling him wouldn't be easy, but once she explained, she knew he'd understand.

Claire pushed her doubts aside and lifted her chin. God had given her a spirit of power, not of fear. That Bible verse she'd looked up just yesterday seemed almost prophetic.

She shoved the door open. "Anyone home?"

The conversation in the other room stilled.

"We're in the living room, Claire," Mrs. Sandy called, an odd note in her voice.

Claire hobbled across the hardwood floor, suddenly missing the walking stick she'd discarded at the edge of the driveway. But she was twenty-eight, not eighty, and a cane was still a cane.

Pausing in front of the beveled mirror, Claire

grimaced at her perspiration-soaked hairline and the streak of dirt across one cheek. She rubbed off the dirt with her fingers and impulsively unclasped her barrette and let the hair fall loose to her shoulders. She ran her hand through it, fluffing the dark strands with her fingers.

She grimaced at her reflection. If only she had time to run upstairs for some quick repair work. Even a dab of lipstick and a touch of powder could do wonders. Nothing gave her more confidence than knowing she looked her best. But at the rate she was walking she'd really be an old woman before she'd make it back.

"Claire, what's—" Mrs. Sandy appeared in the doorway, her carefully controlled expression vanishing at the sight of Claire's ankle. "Oh, my dear. What happened?"

Claire's smile wobbled at Mrs. Sandy's motherly concern. "I fell."

All of a sudden, tears pushed against her lids, and she wanted nothing more than to collapse into the woman's arms.

But she wasn't a schoolgirl and Mrs. Sandy couldn't begin to make everything better. Only Claire could do that. But not if she dissolved in a puddle of tears like a big baby.

She blinked rapidly and swallowed the sob in her throat.

"Oh, honey." Mrs. Sandy looked frantically

around the foyer before pulling a settee across the room and helping Claire to sit.

"Don't move a muscle." Mrs. Sandy's gaze shifted to the doorway leading to the living room. "Tony. Harold. I need your help."

Of course. It was Harold's Fleetwood in the driveway. She'd forgotten this was Mrs. Sandy's big date night.

In an instant the two men stood in the doorway. Still dressed in the dark suit and tie he'd worn for the evening out, Tony looked incredibly handsome. And so strong. So dependable.

Claire smiled.

So angry.

Her smile faded.

Tony leaned against the doorjamb, his arms folded across his chest, and stared, a stony expression on his face.

Mrs. Sandy frowned. "Tony, you're not going to do her much good way over there." Her tone was brusque. "Claire's ankle is hurt and Harold's back isn't the best. You'll need to carry your fiancée into the living room."

Was it only Claire's imagination or did Mrs. Sandy put an extra emphasis on *your fiancée?*

Claire shifted uneasily. She'd thought Tony might be a little irritated. Maybe even a tad bit angry. But it was the pain in his dark eyes that took her by surprise.

"Well, are you going to stand there all day?" Mrs. Sandy said.

Tony straightened and sauntered across the room. When he bent over, Claire wrapped her arms around his neck and inhaled the spicy scent of his cologne, the one he wore for special occasions. She tilted her head and whispered softly against his ear. "There's so much I need to tell you."

"No kidding." Tony didn't even try to keep his voice down.

She stiffened, but he didn't seem to notice. Or care.

It was a relief when he set her in the overstuffed chair.

Mrs. Sandy propped Claire's foot on the ottoman. Harold fetched an ice bag from the kitchen, and the landlady wrapped it carefully around the swollen ankle.

Tony stood aside, facing the fireplace, his back to her.

The tension in the room was so thick you could cut it with a knife. A shiver of fear coursed up Claire's spine. This was worse than she'd imagined.

Finally Harold spoke. "I probably should be going."

"Sit down, Harold," Tony said in a voice she'd never heard before. "Claire wants to tell us about her evening."

"I don't think Harold would be interested." Claire met Tony's firm gaze with an equally direct one of her own. She knew Harold had been instrumental in helping Tony get his job, but she certainly had no intention of discussing this matter in front of him. Or in front of Mrs. Sandy, for that matter. "This is between you and me."

"That's where you're wrong, sweetheart." There was no gentleness in the endearment. "It stopped being between you and me when the deputy stopped by. He told us all about your little adventure."

"I thought I saw his car." Claire stalled for time. She cast a quick glance around the room. "Where's April?"

"In bed." Mrs. Sandy shook her head. "She must have been all tuckered out. I can't remember the last time she went to bed before ten."

"There's no need for her to know about this," Tony said sharply.

"As if I'd want to drag her into it anyway." Claire couldn't keep from bristling at his tone.

"You're the one who brought her up."

I just wanted to make sure she hadn't had a run-in with the deputy.

Claire wanted to tell him if he'd just listen, it would all make sense. But then she realized she couldn't explain what had happened in front of April's mother.

"Is it true?" Tony said. "You were playing strip poker?"

"Yes, but—"

"What were you doing there in the first place?" The muscle in Tony's jaw clenched tight.

"I went to help a friend." That much at least she could admit.

"Which one was your friend?" Tony said, his voice heavy with sarcasm. "Wayne or his brother?"

"Neither." Claire lifted her chin and met his gaze head-on. "She left."

"Who was she? What's her name?"

"I promised I wouldn't say."

"How convenient."

"You don't understand."

"Oh, I understand all too well." Tony shook his head in disgust. "You were having so much fun with two half-naked men that you stayed after this mysterious so-called 'friend' of yours left. Is that the way it was?"

"Yes...I mean no." Claire raked her fingers through her hair. Suddenly nothing made sense. "Believe me. It's not the way it sounds."

"Believe what?" Tony's chin jutted out. "I'll tell you what I believe. I believe that I was stupid for thinking you could actually be happy in a small town with a minister. I believe that when you saw the opportunity for a little fun—granted, not much—you had to take it because life here is not exciting enough for you.''

Claire stared at Tony and wondered if she'd ever really known him. Granted, his pride had been hurt, but was there ever an excuse not to listen to someone you love?

Unless he doesn't love you.

Her breath caught in her throat. Was that what this was about? An excuse? An act? A perfect way to end their fake engagement?

His accusing gaze was riveted on her, and she searched his eyes, looking for even the slightest hint of affection...of love. She found only burning, reproachful eyes.

It all made sense now. But why hadn't he told her this was coming? Prepared her?

Suddenly she was furious. Furious at him. And furious at her vulnerability where he was concerned. For two cents she'd walk out the door and never look back.

But however tempting the thought, Claire couldn't do it. The bottom line was, she owed him. When she'd needed him he'd come through. Regardless of her feelings, she could do no less for him.

She took a deep breath and turned to Harold. ''Mr. Clarke. What kind of job do you think Tony's been doing?''

The man glanced at Tony before shifting his gaze to Claire. "I'm afraid I don't understand."

"Claire, this isn't about me."

Claire waved Tony silent. "I mean, how would you rate him as a minister? Excellent? Good? Fair? Poor?"

"Excellent." Harold's smile told her he was more than willing to change the topic of conversation.

"I imagine you'd like to keep him around awhile?"

"He's got a job here as long as he wants."

Thank You, God.

Claire pretended to adjust the ice bag around her ankle. "I know you were concerned when he first came that he wasn't married. But I think you'd have to agree he's done well in spite of that fact."

"Yes, he has." A puzzled expression blanketed Harold's features. "But I guess I'm not sure what you're getting at."

"Neither am I." Tony's voice was tight with strain.

Only Mrs. Sandy seemed to understand. Her pleading look begged Claire not to take the next step.

Claire moved the ice bag from her ankle and lifted her foot off the ottoman. She clenched her jaw and stood, pain shooting up her leg. Shifting her weight to her other foot, she rested one hand against the top of the chair for support.

"What I'm getting at is that Tony's a great minister, whether he's single or married. One that you'd like to keep."

Harold glanced at Tony and Mrs. Sandy before he nodded. "That's right."

"Good." Claire took a deep breath.

She pulled the heavy diamond from her finger. Her heart clenched. She knew how to play her part. She could do a graceful exit scene. Heaven knows she'd done enough of them in the past.

But never with someone she loved.

Claire shoved the thought aside. It was pointless to love a man who didn't love her back.

"Heads up." She tossed the ring in a high, arching lob.

Tony caught it with ease. He stared at the gem. His brows furrowed. "What's this about?"

"It's over."

"Over?" His stunned expression looked so believable, she almost didn't continue. "Why?"

She wanted to tell him not to play it so real. If he thought it made it easier, he was wrong.

"Why?" Claire forced a careless shrug. She half walked, half hopped to the door, knowing she needed to be able to leave the room once she had said the words so no one could see the truth in her eyes. "Because I don't love you."

She turned and headed down the hall. It was the hardest walk she'd ever taken. The pain in her ankle was nothing compared to the pain in her heart.

Tony stared in stunned disbelief at the ring in his hand. His worst nightmare had come true. She'd found something better and now she was moving on. Just as he thought. Just as he feared.

"Tony, all couples argue." Mrs. Sandy spoke softly. "I'm sure you two will make up."

"No, we won't." Tony shoved the ring into his pocket. Claire was a big-city girl, and despite his background, Tony was now very much a small-town guy. He'd been foolish to think she could love him and his way of life.

"If you'll excuse me." His smile barely lifted his lips, and he knew that it looked forced, but it was the best he could do. "It's been a long day."

Tony could feel their eyes follow him out of the room, but he didn't look back. He couldn't. If he turned, they'd see how he really felt. They'd encourage him to make up with Claire.

The trouble was, they didn't understand what he now understood all too well.

Claire didn't love him. And the worst of it was, he now realized she never had.

Chapter Fifteen

Claire sat alone at the dining room table and took a sip of her coffee. Her bags were packed and she was ready to go. More than ready to blow this town and never look back. Ready to quit hurting every time she caught a glimpse of Tony.

The last two days had been pure torture. Though she'd deliberately tried to avoid him, she hadn't been a hundred percent successful. The times she'd run into him in the halls had been awkward, to say the least.

At least she hadn't had much time to think. She'd offered to help Mrs. Sandy clean the house, and the woman was a demanding taskmaster. They'd scoured the already immaculate two-story from top to bottom in anticipation of the upcoming party.

Mrs. Sandy had originally planned the event to be Claire and Tony's wedding reception, but now it would simply be a Fourth of July blast.

Thankfully she'd be long gone by then. She'd gotten over being mad. She was sure Tony hadn't deliberately set out to hurt her. But he had. And although the anger was gone, the pain remained.

In the past, whenever she'd had a problem with someone she'd bring it to his or her attention in no uncertain terms. But with Tony, it was different. She simply couldn't face him. And, no matter how much she tried, she couldn't stop loving him. If she got too close, she feared he'd see it in her eyes.

Pride was the only thing she had left. If he knew of her feelings, she'd be one of those pathetic creatures she'd always despised, a woman wearing her heart on her sleeve for a man who didn't love her.

Claire cringed and reminded herself it wouldn't be a problem for long. She'd soon be far away from Millville. And Tony.

Strange as it sounded, given the way they parted, she found herself looking forward to seeing her father. It was unfortunate he wouldn't be home when she got there. According to his answering machine he was out of town until next week. She'd surprise him when he got back.

She stared at her bare ring finger and realized her father probably wouldn't be all that surprised to see her. After all, hadn't he been the one who'd

told her she was incapable of sustaining a relationship? That her self-centered personality would
keep her from finding true happiness? Maybe this
time he was right.

But I didn't have a choice.

She'd done everything expected of her. She'd
fulfilled her part of the bargain and she'd changed
in the process. Even she could see she'd become
a much better person and a far cry from the self-
centered, spoiled brat she'd been when she'd arrived in Millville. And it still hadn't worked out.

Claire closed her eyes. Complete and utter mis-
ery washed over her.

*Dear God, I don't pretend to understand Your
will and I know I'm going to have to trust You on
this one. I thought Tony and I made a great team,
but I guess You know best. I do have one request.
It may sound petty, but when You pick a wife for
Tony, could You just not let her be Rachel? I know
she's really involved with Your ministry and she's
probably a good person, but she's not the type of
woman he needs. If You could just trust me on this
one, I'll be forever grateful. Amen.*

Some might say it was wrong to tell God what
to do, but Claire figured she wasn't telling Him
what to do, she was merely offering a suggestion.
God, she knew from past experience, would do just
what He pleased, regardless of her preferences. Af-

ter all, if she had her way Tony would have loved her and they would have lived happily ever after.

But Tony didn't. And instead of heading down the aisle at the end of the week, she was headed out of his life. This time for good.

Tony stared at the clock on his office wall. In less than an hour Claire would leave for Des Moines with Mrs. Sandy, and he'd never see her again.

The despair that had threatened to overwhelm him for the past forty-eight hours returned with a vengeance.

Dear God, please help me to understand and accept Your mysterious ways. I really thought Claire loved me and I truly believed we could have been happy together. I know now that's not Your will. But I have just one suggestion. The Jay Nordstroms of this world may be successful, good-looking guys. They may even be believers, I don't know. But that's not the type of man Claire needs. Trust me on this one. She needs someone....

Tony started, realizing he'd been thinking, ''like me.'' He cleared his throat and continued. *Different. Thank You. Amen.*

Tony rose and moved to the window. The downtown merchants had already started decorating for the Fourth of July festivities.

My wedding day.

He chuckled, but there was no humor in the sound. And despite knowing better, he couldn't quite rid himself of a tiny flicker of hope that until Claire was on the plane to Colorado, there was still a chance.

You're a fool, Karelli. What are you expecting? A miracle?

"Fat chance of that," he muttered.

"Pastor."

Tony whirled at the unexpected voice. "April. What are you doing here?"

The girl stood in the doorway, a suspicious expression on her face. "You were talking to yourself."

"It's a bad habit," Tony said with a self-deprecating grin. He waved her into the office. "Come in and have a seat."

She stepped into the office but made no move to sit down. "We don't have a lot of time."

"For what?"

"Oh, puh-leeze." April heaved an exasperated sigh. "You know."

"No, I don't know. I don't have a clue what you're talking about."

"Okay, I'll spell it out for you." April spoke slowly, articulating each word. "We need to stop my mom from taking Claire to the airport."

"Why would we want to do that?" Tony forced a nonchalant air.

April eyed him with a calculating expression, and he had the strange feeling she could see straight through him.

He averted his gaze and straightened the papers on his desk, shoving a couple of stray pencils into a metal cylinder already filled with pens. When he glanced up, April's gaze was still riveted to him.

"Can't the cleaning wait?" April lifted a brow. "We're talking about something important here."

"April, she *wants* to leave."

"Yeah, right." April scoffed. "Tell that to someone who's stupid enough to believe it."

"She does." He resisted the urge to refill his stapler, or even better yet, leave the room. "Small-town living isn't for her."

And neither am I.

Tony shoved his hands into his pockets, his fingers curving around his grandmother's ring. He pulled it from his pocket and glanced at the sparkling gem.

He'd left the diamond on the dresser the past two days instead of putting it into the safety deposit box where it belonged.

It belongs on Claire's finger.

This morning Tony couldn't stand looking at it any longer. He'd scooped it up, along with some spare change, and put it in his pocket to get it out of sight. But all day it had been a constant reminder of what he was losing.

"I don't know why you think Claire wants to leave," April said with more than a hint of impatience. "She's told me plenty of times how much she liked it here."

Tony marveled at her youthful optimism and wished his own hadn't been washed away in the harsh sea of reality. He dropped the ring into his pocket.

"April, this is her decision. *She* broke up with *me*." The fact that she could walk away so easily still hurt.

"Did you ever tell her you loved her? That you wanted her to stay?"

"A lot has gone on in the last couple of days. I really don't want to dis—"

"Tell me you're not talking about that thing at the Nordstrom place."

"How'd you find out about that?"

"Is that why she's leaving?" she asked.

"It might have something to do with it." He shrugged. He certainly wasn't going to discuss his personal life with a seventeen-year-old.

"What did she say happened that night?"

"She claimed she'd gone to help a friend."

"And?"

"That's it. We didn't discuss it further." Tony shook his head, trying to erase the vivid picture the officer had painted. "I heard all I needed to know from the deputy."

"You've got to be kidding."

Tony remained silent. As far as he was concerned, this discussion was closed.

"You aren't kidding." Amazement sounded in her voice. She shook her head. "All I can say is it's a good thing God doesn't operate the way you do."

"What do you mean?" Tony said.

"You keep saying God is there for us. He listens to our troubles. He's our friend, no matter what." April's gaze flicked over Tony, and he could see the disappointment in her eyes. "You talk in your sermons about how we should follow God's example. I guess you don't practice what you preach. I guess you don't mean the things you tell the rest of us about being there for each other."

"April." Tony fought to hold on to his temper.

"What if I told you *I* was Claire's friend? The one she helped that night?"

Tony started to say she couldn't be, but when he stared into her clear blue eyes, he knew she was telling him the truth.

But why hadn't she said anything before? Why now?

He took a deep steadying breath, pulled up a chair and gestured for her to take the other. "Why don't you tell me what happened that night?"

She sat down reluctantly. Beads of perspiration dotted her forehead. "Okay, but this is just be-

tween you, me and Claire,'' April said. ''You can't
tell anybody else, especially my mom.''

Tony paused. He didn't like keeping things from
a parent, but in his heart he knew if Claire thought
the secret was something Mrs. Sandy needed to
know, she would have never promised not to tell.
''I won't say a word.''

She flashed him a grateful smile, folded her
hands in her lap almost as if she were praying and
took a deep breath.

A few minutes later Tony sat back in his chair,
stunned by April's revelation. He could only imagine what Claire had gone through. No wonder her
beautiful face had been lined with stress that night.
At the time, he hadn't given it a second thought.
He'd been too caught up in his own concerns.

Thank You, Father, for keeping her safe.

''Why didn't she tell me all this?'' he asked, but
he knew the answer. *Because I wouldn't listen.*

''I don't know.'' April lifted one shoulder in a
halfhearted shrug. ''She told me she was going to,
said she didn't want there to be any secrets between the two of you. I was cool with her telling
you. I just made her promise not to tell anyone
else.''

There's so much I need to tell you.

He thought of how he'd interrogated Claire in
front of Harold and Mrs. Sandy. No wonder she'd

kept silent. Tony ran a shaky hand through his hair. He'd really botched this one.

"Can I go now?"

"Of course." His gaze met hers. "Thanks for telling me, April."

"Yeah, well, you needed to know." She stood and walked to the door, but instead of opening it, she turned back, one hand still on the knob. "Claire's a good person. She saved my life."

April turned on her heel. Before he could say a word, the door slammed behind her.

Tony stood there for the longest time. The enormity of what he'd done washed over him in ever increasing waves of guilt and recrimination. He sank into the chair and covered his face with his hands.

He'd always prided himself on being a good man. A caring man. A man of God. But when it counted most, when it came time to put his words into action, he'd failed. April had been right about that, too.

From the mouths of babes...

A deep sense of shame filled him. Since she'd arrived in town, Claire had never given him any reason to doubt her. But when he thought back, that's all he had done. He'd tested her at every opportunity, waiting for her to disappoint him. And, when this latest episode occurred, it had almost been a relief to have his low expectations validated.

He'd gotten what he deserved. He'd lost the woman he loved. But Claire had *not* deserved what she'd gotten.

She'd tried to explain.

He'd refused to listen.

And all the time he'd thought only of himself. Now he needed to make things right with her. At the very least apologize and ask for forgiveness. But how could he face her?

God has not given us a spirit of fear. But He has given us a spirit of power and love.

The Bible verse from Timothy ran through his head.

Tony took a deep breath and headed for the door. This time he wasn't going to let fear or foolish pride stand in the way of doing the right thing.

"If you want to leave early, I'm—" The words died in Claire's throat. It wasn't the landlady who'd come into the dining room, but Tony. She set her book facedown on the table. "If you're looking for Mrs. Sandy, I haven't seen her."

He shifted from one foot to the other, but his gaze didn't waver. "Actually I was looking for you."

"Really?" She lifted a brow. "I didn't think

you wanted to see me. You've spent the last few days avoiding me like I had the plague.''

He ignored the flippant comment and pulled out a chair opposite her. "Care if I sit down?''

"Suit yourself." Claire took a sip of her cold coffee. "I'm getting ready to leave soon anyway."

"I've got a couple of things I want to talk to you about." Tony folded his hands on the table in front of him, and his expression grew serious. "Can you spare a few minutes?"

Claire made a show of glancing at her watch. "I suppose. If you make it short."

"This won't take long." Tony drew a deep breath. "First, I'm really sorry about the other night. I never even gave you a chance to explain."

"You're right. You didn't," Claire said, proud she could sound so offhand when her insides churned. "But that's the past. It doesn't matter now. Let's just drop it."

"I can't." He cleared his throat, and a hint of red crept up his neck. "The way I talked to you was inexcusable."

"You're right," she said. "It was."

"I want you to understand why I acted that way."

"C'mon, Tony, get real." She forced another sip of the coffee down her throat. "I already figured out what was going on."

"You did?" Surprise sounded in his voice.

"I'm not stupid." Claire picked up the book and read the same sentence for the third time. "But like I said, it doesn't matter now."

"It does to me," Tony said. "I can't begin to tell you how sorry I am you had to go through that alone. On the other hand, I thank God you were there for her."

She stared at him for a long moment. "So, how much did April tell you?"

"Everything," Tony said. "I feel terrible. I wouldn't blame you if you never speak to me again."

"Never is a long time." Claire eyed him calculatingly. He seemed repentant. And he did look truly gorgeous in those khaki pants and navy polo. Perhaps she should cut him a little slack. "Actually, I have to hand it to you. You took advantage of a heaven-sent opportunity. I'd probably have done the exact same thing."

"I'm not sure I follow what you're saying."

"C'mon, you don't have to pretend. I know the score. You'd found the perfect way for us to break up and you took it. Although," she added, "it would have been nice if you'd warned me."

"Perfect way to break up?" His brow furrowed. "What are you talking about? I never wanted to break up with you. I wanted to marry you."

"Marry me?" Her normally husky voice came

out as a squeak. She cleared her throat. "Have you been drinking the communion wine?"

"I'm totally sober." His gaze met hers. "And I mean every word."

"Our engagement was just an act, a show for the church board to keep your job. You don't love me."

"Of course, I love you. I wouldn't want to marry you if I didn't," Tony said. "You're the one who doesn't love me."

"Who says I don't?" The words popped out of her mouth before she could stop them.

A strange gleam flickered in his eyes, and she could almost see the wheels turning in his head. That incredible dimple flashed in his cheek. "Claire Waters, are you saying you *do* love me?"

"Are you saying *you* love *me?*" Claire said.

"That's exactly what I'm saying."

She'd be putting her heart on the line.

Taking a risk he'd break it again.

Stubborn pride.

She lifted her chin and sniffed. "Call me crazy, but I love you, too."

Their eyes locked and their breathing came in unison. Claire's heart hammered against her ribs.

Tony reached across the table and brushed her cheek with his knuckles. The mere touch of his hand sent a warm shiver through her. Thick with emotion, his voice shook slightly. "I love you more than anything."

She hesitated, unable to believe that just when she'd given up hope, her dream was coming true. "If you're playing with me..."

"I'd like to," he said with a wicked grin, "but we've got to wait until we're married for that."

Claire smiled, finally convinced. A languid warmth filled her limbs at the thought of their wedding night. Her breathing picked up speed. "I don't suppose you have a date in mind."

"As a matter of fact I do." His eyes glittered, looking more black than brown. "Independence Day is coming up, and I've always been partial to that holiday. Maybe it's because I've always liked firecrackers."

"Firecrackers can blow up unexpectedly," Claire said with an impish grin. "Sometimes right in your face."

"Sometimes that's just what a foolish minister deserves." He chuckled. "There's one other thing." Tony rose and rounded the table, pulling her to her feet. "We need to seal this deal with a kiss."

He brushed a piece of hair from her face with the back of his hand. It was a tender gesture, gentle and loving, matching the soft look in his eyes. "What do you say, sweetheart? Can I kiss you?"

She stared at this man she loved more than life itself and lifted her lips to his. "Anytime..."

The word was muffled by the crush of his lips against hers. She wrapped her arms around his neck.

"Oh, my." Mrs. Sandy tittered. "Does this mean you're not leaving for Colorado and that the wedding is back on?"

Tony groaned under his breath. Claire turned in his arms to face the landlady, unable to keep the smile from her lips. "That's just what it means."

"Thank goodness." The landlady heaved a relieved sigh. "I was hoping he didn't make the trip for nothing."

Puzzled, Claire glanced at Tony, but he just shrugged. "I guess I don't understand. Who are you talking about?"

"Why, your father, of course," Mrs. Sandy said. "I invited him to the wedding, and there's a message on the recorder. He just landed in Des Moines and he's on his way here."

"You invited him to the wedding?" Claire said. "How did you even find him?"

"You gave me his number." A hint of pink colored Mrs. Sandy's cheeks. "To use in case of an emergency. You said he was a very busy man, but I figured a daughter getting married is sort of an emergency. And he was thrilled with the news. Simply thrilled. You're not mad, are you?"

Claire shook her head. Talk about mysterious ways. Having her father there to walk her down the aisle would be a dream come true. "Actually, that's wonderful."

"He should be getting here about the same time as my parents and grandmother. Looks like tonight will be a family dinner," Tony said, his arm resting lightly around Claire's waist.

"Oh, my goodness." Mrs. Sandy eyes widened. "I'll need to thaw out another steak. If you two will excuse me."

The minute the woman left the room, Claire turned to Tony with a smile, her lips already tingling in anticipation. "Now, where were we?"

"First things first." Tony brushed a kiss across her lips, stepped back and reached into his pocket. "The relatives are going to expect you to be—" he held out his hand palm upward "—wearing my ring."

Claire's breath caught in her throat. Reverently she reached for the gem.

He shook his head and smiled. "Let me."

With great care he slid it on her finger.

"Oh, Tony." She held out her hand, admiring the diamond she'd once despised.

"We don't have time to shop for another one before the wedding," Tony said. "But this fall we'll take a trip, wherever you want, and you can pick out the ring of your dreams."

"I don't think so."

Tony raised a brow. "I promise. We—"

"I want this ring."

"But it's flawed." His brows pulled together in confusion. "You said so yourself."

"I know," Claire said, "but so are you, and I still love you."

His lips quirked upward. "Gee, thanks."

"Okay. Maybe I'm not perfect, either," she said with mock resignation. "But together we have this great thing, this…perfect love."

"Perfect?"

"Okay," she said with a saucy smile. "Maybe not perfect, but good."

"Very good," Tony said.

His eyes darkened, and when his lips met hers, Claire closed her eyes and kissed him, losing herself in the surge of emotion that exploded inside her like fireworks on the Fourth of July.

Their lives would be filled with fireworks.

On their wedding day tomorrow.

And all the days to come.

* * * * *

Dear Reader,

If you've read my third novel for Love Inspired,
The Marrying Kind, then you've already met Tony and
Claire. When I first started writing *The Marrying Kind*,
I had no intention of bringing Tony and Claire back in a
book of their own. But the closer I got to the end of that
book, the more I realized that I hadn't seen the last of
Claire Waters. She demanded a book of her own!

Although you may find her a rather unlikely heroine at
the beginning of this story, I hope that you'll agree with
me that she is totally "redeemable."

I enjoyed writing this book and I hope you like reading
it!

Cynthia Rutledge

Next Month
From Steeple Hill's

Love Inspired

A GROOM WORTH WAITING FOR

by *Crystal Stovall*

Jilted at the altar by her fiancé, Amy Jenkins vows to start a new life in Lexington, Kentucky. But her plans go terribly awry when she's held up in a convenience store robbery! Having survived the attack thanks to a dynamic stranger, she finds herself drawn deeply into Matthew Wynn's life. Does God's plan for her future include finding in Matthew a groom worth waiting for?

Don't miss
A GROOM WORTH WAITING FOR
On sale November 2001

Love Inspired

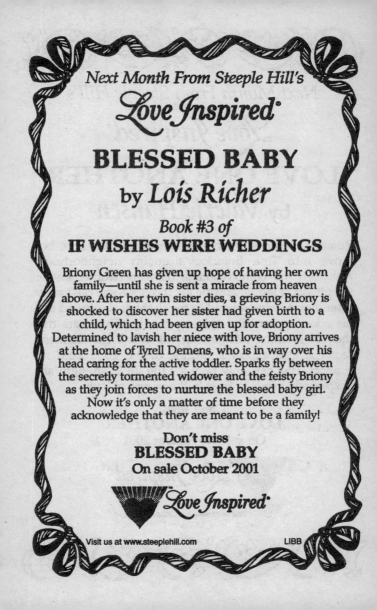

Next Month From Steeple Hill's

Love Inspired®

LOVE ONE ANOTHER
by *Valerie Hansen*

Romance blooms when Zac Frazier and his little boy move into Tina Braddock's quaint neighborhood. Although the compassionate day-care worker knows the pitfalls of letting anyone get too close, she can't resist extending a helping hand to the dashing single dad and his adorable son. But a heavy-hearted Tina fears that their blossoming relationship will wilt if her shameful secret is ever exposed. Turning to the good Lord for support, Tina can only pray for the inner strength she desperately needs to trust in the power of love....

Don't miss
LOVE ONE ANOTHER
On sale November 2001

Love Inspired®